THE
OLD CADET

THE
OLD CADET

D. S. COOPER

For more information:
www.dscooperbooks.com

Cover design by Ebook Launch
www.ebooklaunch.com

Book design by Maureen Cutajar
www.gopublished.com

Print ISBN: 978-0-9909743-5-2
Ebook ISBN: 978-0-9909743-4-5

For the Class of 1969

A distant rifle shot cracked across a forested hillside in central Pennsylvania.

The State Police gave chase, but the boy ran down long-forgotten paths through the dense forest and slipped unseen into a dormitory at Ethan North Academy.

"You can't get away with it," his roommate said as the boy hid his .22 rifle under his bunk.

"You're the only one who knows," the boy said, when he hid his muddy sneakers and sat across from the roommate at their desk. He opened his *Literature of England* book to *Beowulf*. "If we stick together ... like always ... they'll never prove I did it."

"We'll take the secret to the grave," the roommate smiled.

TWENTY YEARS LATER

CHAPTER 1

THE OLD GUARD

"Why do people do this weird stuff?"

"I don't know, Murph." Lieutenant Kevin O'Connor glanced across the cab of the Bomb Squad truck at his partner. "Maybe we can disarm this device and collar the guy. Then you can ask him in person."

"That'd be good. Before he hurts somebody."

Driving the squad's big truck was not really the lieutenant's job. But Kevin O'Connor loved wheeling the black behemoth through Boston's narrow streets, coming within inches of cars, with the diesel engine growling and the siren yelping. It was his way of relaxing before walking up on a high-explosive device.

Their destination was deep in the North End, in a warren of ancient brick buildings cut by narrow cobblestone streets. He parked their rig as close as he could, but they'd still have to walk the last fifty yards.

Patrol officers were moving the barricades back when the men in black uniforms stepped out of the truck. It was a long way down from the cab, but even with his gun belt on, O'Connor landed lightly, with his heavy flak vest and helmet in a bag slung over his shoulder. He still ran five miles every other day, so he was in better shape than some thirty-eight-year-old cops.

A familiar WBZ newswoman and her cameraman appeared alongside the rig.

"The elite Bomb Squad is just arriving." She stepped closer and turned the microphone to Kevin, "Lieutenant, is there any connection to terrorism?"

"I'm kind of busy right now, Louisa. You might want to get behind the barricades, for your own safety."

"Did you hear that?" Murph asked as they walked up the cobblestones, carrying flak vests and helmets. "We're elite."

"Yeah," Kevin laughed.

The Elite Bomb Squad. Even though they were just ordinary cops doing a specialized job. And other than in their name, "bomb" was a word which the squad members never used. They dealt with "devices"—sometimes, clever devices.

The first responders and the young woman who had discovered the suspicious package were waiting a few doors down.

"What have you got?" Lieutenant O'Connor asked the first officer on the scene, who stood at the center of a huddle of sergeants and lieutenants.

"A shoe box on the third-floor landing. Miss Duarte found it in front of her door when she got home from MIT. When she lifted the cover, it looked like there was a length of iron pipe inside."

"What's your field, Miss?" he searched her eyes for deceit but saw only fear and confusion.

"Chemistry. I'm writing my thesis now."

Kevin looked at Murph. *That's interesting.*

"I'll buy you dinner if one of her undergrad students isn't our bad guy," Kevin offered as they walked towards her apartment.

"Yeah. That's all we need, some smart-ass little college kid playing against us. Five will get you ten, he's a sexually frustrated little geek."

They put on their flak vests and helmets when they approached the steps to the front door. The old three-story house was irregularly shaped and wedged between other structures on the sloping and curved street. They walked up two flights of narrow, winding steps together, but Lieutenant O'Connor was always the first to enter the danger zone. So he went up the last floor by himself. The final steps were steeper, irregularly spaced, and curving.

"Just like the one at Fanule Hall," he told Murph, when he came down. "Looks like a pipe unit with a trembler trigger."

"One thing's for sure," Murph said, "we'll never get the robot up here. This is going to be old school."

"Wouldn't have it any other way," Kevin smiled.

They went downstairs and walked to the squad truck. The transporter truck with the big steel containment sphere had arrived by then, along with the other members of the unit.

"There's not enough room to work on the stairway," Lieutenant O'Connor began. "We're going to have to go at it from inside the apartment. Let's get the fire service to put the snorkel up to a window. We'll go into the apartment that way and use a manipulator pole to swing the door open from inside."

"Yeah, yeah," Murph laughed. "I'll flip you for the honors."

O'Connor tossed a quarter.

"Are you kidding? Not again!" Murph laughed as he began donning the full-body blast suit. "Make sure they spell my name right in the obituary, okay?"

Kevin helped Murph into the basket of the snorkel truck. A fireman was going to ride up with him.

"I'll be on the second-floor landing," Kevin said.

"Okay. But you should suit up."

"Like I could climb the stairs in a full suit," Kevin muttered. "I'll be around the corner. Just don't fumble the damn thing down the stairs into my lap, okay?"

Murph went into the apartment through the window. He opened the front door from inside the apartment with a long pole, standing well clear. Then he rigged a small cannon alongside the device, containing a slug of water in a condom and a blank 12-gauge shotgun shell. Murph was outside the window in the snorkel basket when they fired the disrupter cannon.

"Fire in the hole ... Fire in the hole ... Fire in the hole!"

Kevin O'Connor stood on the second-floor landing. He thought that he would be far enough from the device to avoid injury, just in case it detonated when Murph fired the water cannon.

He was wrong.

The explosion was incredibly loud, but mostly, Kevin saw a yellow-green flash and felt his body falling through the air, hurtling down the stairs. When the smoke cleared, he was facedown on the first floor. He had landed hard, on his knees. He tried to roll over, but it felt as if his legs were gone.

The pain, when it came, was reassuring. It was good pain. Wonderful pain. His legs were still attached.

"Hang in there, Lieutenant," a fireman said as they put him in the ambulance. "We're taking you to Mass General Hospital. Do you know what MGH really stands for?"

Kevin O'Connor was dazed but conscious throughout, and he shook his head no.

"Mankind's Greatest Hospital. You're all set, buddy."

"On behalf of the board of governors, I demand that you take this ship back to port immediately!"

Doctor Walter Weiss looked at the seasick trustee of the University of Rhode Island, who was waving an accusatory finger in his face. The sea was nearly flat calm, and the deck of the *R/V Hope* was barely moving. The deep submersible vehicle with a clear acrylic dome for two passengers was sitting on the stern, ready to dive five hundred fathoms into Block Canyon on the southern edge of the Continental Shelf.

"Our field study plan calls for one more dive," Doctor Weiss calmly said, drilling into the trustee with his eyes. "I'm going on this one myself."

"It's ridiculous, you being out here in the first place. The dean of Oceanography should be in his office."

"This is my office," Walter Weiss replied as he twisted his tall frame into the acrylic sphere at the front of the deep submersible. Taking off his ball cap and putting on a communications headset revealed thinning brown hair on the top of his head.

"Here we go," the young woman piloting the submersible said when they were lowered over the stern and the sea enveloped their acrylic cocoon. As they sank, she turned to Doctor Weiss.

"So, Captain Ahab, we're going to find your white whale, aren't we?"

"Am I that transparent?" Walter Weiss smiled.

"Everybody on the boat—except the trustee—knows the true purpose of the last dive of every voyage to Block Canyon."

"If the board of governors has their way, I may not have many last dives left."

"Well, what did you expect, Doc? Your lecture at the Academy of Science has caused a brouhaha at the university."

"That's what lectures are supposed to do."

"You fired a broadside at the environmentalists."

"I simply said that they are promoting an emotional response to a geopolitical problem."

"I'm sorry, but didn't you say that climate change is real and irreversible, and that conservation is not the answer to the problem? That the free and open societies of the world have a moral obligation to grow and prosper in the face of declining resources?"

"That's a fair summation of my thesis. We can't do any good in the world if we impoverish ourselves."

"That's heresy," she tapped the depth gauge as they descended into darkness. "What about the underprivileged people of the world?"

"They are underprivileged because their societies don't work, not because they lack resources. Keeping my home's thermostat at sixty-four degrees rather than seventy-two degrees is not going to solve their problems. We need to help them fix their societies, not hobble our own."

"But … the Sierra Club and the Audubon Society are calling for your head. Green Peace wants you prosecuted by the World Court at The Hague."

"It's wonderful, isn't it? As a scientist and an educator, that's the sort of response you dream of."

They landed on a sandy slope, strewn with boulders. The deep sea beyond their floodlights was blue-green and then black farther away.

"Down some more?" The young sub-pilot asked.

"Yes. And a few meters to the east please, Kelly."

"Hello," she said, when the wreck of the fishing boat appeared in their lights.

"Good job, Kelly. Let's work our way to the other side."

"Sure. Just help me look out for nets and cables, especially behind us. This thing is a snag waiting to happen."

"You bet I will."

"So, what is it?" Kelly wanted to know as she deftly used the thrusters. "Why do you keep coming back to this old wreck of a fishing boat, when you're supposed to be researching the geography of the Continental Shelf?"

"This isn't any fishing boat. This is the *Four Brothers*, out of Point Judith."

"Sure," Kelly nodded. "Lost with all hands, thirty-two years ago. Cause unknown."

"Not exactly unknown, Kelly. This vessel was struck by a ship."

"Okay. Although some people think they picked up an old torpedo or depth charge in their nets."

"Perhaps. But I've seen enough to believe that a much larger vessel ran the *Four Brothers* down. If the wreck keeps shifting and sliding deeper down the slope, eventually we'll get a good look at the damage to her port side."

"Well, we can almost see the port side now. But I don't think we dare get any closer."

"Darn it," Doctor Weiss muttered. "Look at that fragment of steel under the hull. That could easily have a paint sample if we grasped it with the mechanical arm."

"Well, maybe we could get a bit closer. Only because you're my favorite dive partner."

"That's the spirit!"

She inched the submarine closer. The thrusters stirred up plumes of sand and mud from the bottom. Then a saucer-sized, hunk of steel hull plating was in the grasp of the mechanical arm.

"Brilliant!" Doctor Weiss tapped her shoulder. "At last!"

"Now all we have to do is get out of here."

When she used the thrusters to back away, nothing happened.

"Uh-oh," Kelly uttered as she amped-up the thruster motors. A cloud of sand billowed in front of the sub, but they didn't move.

"Darn it," Doctor Weiss said, turning to look behind the sub. "That cable behind us must have been buried in the sand."

"Okay," she shut down all of the thrusters. "Let's just let everything settle down and see what we've got."

When the clouds of dust in front of their clear dome cleared, they saw that an old fishing net from the *Four Brothers* had settled on both mechanical arms at the front of the sub, as well.

"Oh, boy," Kelly said. "Snagged at both ends. I knew I should have stayed in my bunk today."

"Yup," Doctor Weiss chuckled, "we are proverbially screwed, aren't we?"

They spent about an hour trying to free the mechanical arms from the net, without success. Finally, Kelly turned to Doctor Weiss with her plan.

"We have to jettison the manipulator arms, Doc."

"Do what you have to do, Captain."

"Okay, here goes."

Kelly pulled the pins and raised the plungers to disconnect the hydraulic power pack and the mechanical arms from under their dome at the front of the sub.

"There goes a few million bucks," she sighed.

"And my paint sample," Doctor Weiss moaned.

When Kelly turned the submarine around, the mechanical front section remained on the bottom like the severed claws of a lobster.

"Let's hope we don't have to separate the sphere," she whispered.

"God, no!" Doctor Weiss agreed.

When she pulled ahead, it became apparent that the stern of the submersible was hopelessly tangled in a heavy cable.

"We're stuck," Kelly admitted.

"Too bad the Navy's NR-1 isn't in New London anymore," Walter Weiss rued. "They could get us out of here before we run out of air."

"We only have one choice," Kelly said. "Separate the sphere."

"Theoretically, we would shoot to the surface in this acrylic co-coon," he nodded. "Let's do it."

Kelly reached down and pulled the safety pins from the release handle. She gripped the lever in her hand but didn't move.

"I … can't do it," her words came heavy with emotion. "This has never been tried before. There are a thousand things that can go wrong. We might not live through this ascent."

Walter Weiss put his hand on hers.

"It'll be okay, Kelly. Let's both pull this lever, together. Ready?"

———

Colonel Arthur C. W. Hammond III still made a complete tour of the campus of Ethan North Military Academy every day, even though it was the end of September, and for the first time in one hundred and sixteen years, no cadets were present in the dormitories or classrooms. Two hundred chairs sat empty under the art-deco lamps hanging from the high ceiling in the dining hall, and the grass on the athletic fields waited expectantly for youthful footfalls which would not come.

Colonel Hammond began his solo inspection around the circle of brick buildings each day from Founders Hall, where his office and the dining room were located. His steps were a march, befitting a West Point graduate. Chin up, back always perfectly erect. First, over to the junior school, grades 6 through 8. Then up to Building '51 at the foot of Dynamite Mountain, with dormitory rooms upstairs and classrooms and a science laboratory below. Next, down to the gym and the library. He often climbed the six stories into the bell tower atop the library, which offered a panoramic view of the campus and the town of New Manor, even though the clockwork bells had been silenced the year before, after the last cadet had withdrawn from the school. Then through the Gables and Eagle Hall, past the cannon on the quad, and into the chapel.

It was there that Arthur "Trip" Hammond paused for a long moment of quiet reflection. Until the double doors under the balcony burst open and Rocky Chambers came striding down the aisle between the pews, bellowing a greeting.

"Trip! How the hell are you?"

Colonel Arthur C. W. Hammond III bowed his head.

"Good morning, Rocky."

"What are we praying for today?" Rocky asked as he leaped over the back of a pew to land seated alongside his old friend.

Such gymnastics were an amazing feat for a man in his early seventies. But Master Sergeant Rocky Chambers was as ageless as he was irreverent. He had graduated from Ethan North a few years ahead of Arthur Hammond III, and he'd chosen the path of a career enlisted man rather than West Point. Along the way he had become a combat veteran, a motorcycle racer, and an amateur boxing champion with a college degree.

When his return to teach at Ethan North Academy didn't work out, Rocky had bought a farm and worked in the New Manor public schools.

"I was just wondering," Colonel Hammond muttered, "how my father and grandfather kept the school open with full admissions for so many years."

"You were doing okay yourself, Trip. Until the Chinese kid wandered off."

"I suppose. For one hundred and fifteen years, we never even had a student seriously injured during the school year. Oh, there were some broken bones and one nasty sledding accident up on Dynamite. But nothing a stay in the infirmary couldn't handle."

"Other than Ethan North himself," Rocky pointed out. "As we all know, General Jacob North came home from the Spanish-American

War and renamed the school after his own young son, who'd fallen off the Little Juniata railroad trestle while he was away."

"Yes … although I now sometimes regret that my grandfather took over after General North passed away without an heir."

Trip Hammond raised his head and looked at his wristwatch.

"She'll be here soon."

"I know," Rocky nodded.

"She's here every day now, you know. She left her condo in Georgetown and took a furnished room over Barton's store, to be near Jonathan."

"Fine," Rocky stood up. "Come on, Trip. I'll walk up to Founders Hall with you."

They walked among the giant elms on the campus and climbed the granite steps framed by white columns on the pediment of Founders Hall. Colonel Hammond sat at the president's desk, with Rocky nearby.

Liu Chen arrived only a few minutes later, with her eternal question.

"Have you found Jonathan today?"

"No."

"Then why aren't you out looking?"

It seemed pointless to mention that the State Police and the FBI, augmented by hundreds of local volunteers, had spent months searching for her son. His disappearance had also attracted the usual mystics, seers and psychics, as well as an amateur "search and recovery" organization in snazzy jumpsuits, which seemed more bent on fundraising and self-aggrandizement than actually locating sixteen-year-old Jonathan Chen.

"Actually, Miss Chen, one of our most distinguished alumni has agreed to come and take a second look at the quarry. Doctor Weiss is one of the country's foremost oceanographers."

"Doctor Walter Weiss?"

"You know the name?"

"Of course. I'm a scientific grant writer, and Doctor Weiss is getting quite a bit of bad press in academic circles as of late. His science is sound, but his conclusions about eco-politics are laughable. And he recently destroyed a multimillion-dollar submersible on a reckless boondoggle to look at some old fishing boat on the seafloor. He's hardly the sort of man to help locate Jonathan."

"Nonetheless, he may be able to help us with a more thorough underwater search of the quarry."

"What about this hunter whom people speak of? I've been told that he actually knew the mountain man, and even visited his camp frequently."

"You mean Derek Yeager? He certainly spent more time on Dynamite than most cadets. But that was twenty years ago, Miss Chen. And despite occasional sightings, the idea of a mountain man living behind the campus is almost certainly a myth. Boomer is simply the creation of overactive teenage minds."

"The searchers found old campsites," Liu Chen insisted.

She appeared to be too young to have a sixteen-year-old son. With long black hair and prominent round cheekbones, which were ripe from the sun. She stood in front of the two men with a relaxed stance, perfectly erect, with her hands hanging at her sides.

"He won't come," Rocky interjected. "Derek Yeager hates this place."

"How is that?"

"There were some discipline problems," Colonel Hammond spread his hands and sighed. "I had to expel him. Two weeks before he was due to graduate."

"Let me talk to him. This Boomer character could be holding Jonathan captive."

"It wouldn't do any good. Derek vowed never to set foot on the campus again. And I'm not sure that I would want him here. He can be quite disruptive."

"You lost my son. My only child. He walked into the woods and disappeared. Perhaps one of Derek Yeager's classmates could appeal to his better instincts?"

"His old roommate would be the only one for that task," Rocky said. "But Kevin O'Connor is in no shape to help anyone, right now."

"He was killed, wasn't he?" Colonel Hammond's brow narrowed. "That Boston bombing affair?"

"Not so," Rocky shook his head. "But his injuries were horrific. Last I heard, he was in long-term rehabilitation."

"Then I'll call the hunter myself," Liu Chen was determined. "I demand his contact information, please!"

Rocky dug through his wallet and pulled out a frayed and worn business card.

"Derek Yeager," Liu Chen read, when she had the card in her hand. "Alaskan Hunter."

"That's him."

"Alaska?"

"Yes. And good luck getting him down to the lower forty-eight."

———

"He's magnificent!"

They were prone on a slope strewn with loose stone, peering over the rim. The speaker was the CEO of a major corporation. A power-house in the world of finance. But to Derek Yeager, he was another overweight and out-of-shape client who had arrived at his hunting camp with a rifle, which was not sighted-in for the ranges necessary to take sheep in the mountains, and fancy new expedition clothing, which was more suited to Madison Avenue than the Brooks Range.

"No. He's tired and old," Derek muttered, peering through binoculars. "Take your shot."

"Okay. But it won't be easy in this cold," the man complained.

Derek knew that the man's modern fabrics were nearly useless when lying down on damp rocks. His own outermost layer was a loose-fitting oiled canvas poncho, over dungarees and a wool jacket and long johns.

"This damn sling is getting in the way."

"Just take the shot," Derek whispered. He had made the man add the sling to carry his rifle on his shoulder rather than in his hands when moving on the loose stones.

Derek could see that the muzzle of the rifle was wandering. Making random, uncontrolled movements, while the man vacillated.

This is the ram's last season, Derek thought. *He'll starve this winter.*

"Anytime now," Derek whispered. "He won't stand still forever."

The barrel of the .300 Weatherby was making even more random movements.

He'll take a wild shot and wound the ram, Derek realized. *This clumsy billionaire isn't worthy of the trophy kill.*

Derek Yeager rose up on his shoulder and intentionally hit the ram's eyes with a reflection off the binoculars. The cagey old animal leaped ahead, and the client's shot missed and sent loose rocks flying.

"Damn it!"

"Tough break, Richard."

"We'll get another one, right?"

"No. I promised you a shot. You missed."

"We can go over the next ridge, and see what's there."

"No, we can't. Because you can't move quickly and quietly enough. I offered you a shot at a ram. You missed."

"I paid eight thousand dollars for this?"

"Yes, you did," Derek said, standing and picking up his gear. "In advance."

"You can't treat me this way, Yeager."

"You mean you still think you get special treatment because you're a big wheel on Wall Street? Tell it to the mountains. They don't care what you do in the city."

"I'll ruin you."

"Sure," Derek stopped walking and turned back to the man. "Go back to camp and tell your rich friends you were too out of shape and a lousy shot. Or, tell them you had a tough and challenging hunt, but didn't get the trophy. I don't care, either way."

The two men walked for an hour before they climbed into Derek's Super Cub airplane for the flight back to camp. He took off from a gravel bar alongside the river and flew below the mountain ridges back to his camp's landing strip.

"It was a great hunt!" the billionaire CEO told the other men in his party at Derek's camp.

"We tried," Derek shrugged. "We missed."

"Next year," the man said as he was getting on the chartered float plane for the trip back to Anchorage.

"Like hell," Derek muttered after the float plane lifted off.

When Derek got back to his cabin, the satellite phone was beeping. The caller was a woman.

"Mister Derek Yeager? My name is Liu Chen, and I need your services."

"No more hunting this year. It's too late in the season."

The only reason he didn't hang up immediately was that he liked her voice.

"My son is missing."

"What? He's missing in Alaska?"

"No. In Pennsylvania."

"Well, I don't know why that would concern me. But go on."

"My son is sixteen years old. Jonathan was a cadet at Ethan North Academy. Last May, he walked into the forest on Dynamite Mountain, and he has not been seen since."

"That's too bad."

"They tell me that you are the only one who ever knew the mountain man. The one they call Boomer."

"Lady … are you kidding me? Boomer was at least forty or fifty years old when I saw him, and that was twenty years ago. He's dead by now, or off the mountain."

"Please come, Mister Yeager."

"Listen, this is a satellite phone. Calls are expensive."

"I'll pay your usual daily guide rate plus travel and all expenses."

"I don't go to the lower forty-eight that often."

"One of your friends is coming. An oceanographer."

"Walt Weiss? He was a few years ahead of me in school. I didn't know him all that well."

"Mister Yeager, my Jonathan also spoke with this man Boomer. He wrote about it in a letter to me, one week before he disappeared."

"That's … really something. If it's true."

"Yes. Jonathan did not lie. So you can come?"

"Well, a friend's widow did ask me to fly his Cessna Skywagon south to be sold."

"So you will come? Soon?"

Her voice is alluring, Derek thought. *And if she'll pay…*

"Okay. But first I have to take care of something."

Derek Yeager knew that he couldn't leave the old ram out there. He would fly back to the gravel bar in the river in the morning and trot along the ridges with his rifle slung. He would carry only enough to possibly survive the night if the weather turned against him. But he would get his shot, and he would not miss.

CHAPTER 2

THE HOLY GROUND

Kevin O'Connor was sleeping until the train came out of the tunnel into sudden daylight. He knew, from having made the same trip on the Pennsylvania Railroad so often during his school years, that the train had crossed the Susquehanna and Little Juniata Rivers and passed through Kettle Mountain into Parsons County.

"New Manor next stop," the conductor said, when he found Kevin. "I'll meet you at the back of the car, sir."

Kevin forgot the damage to his right shoulder until he couldn't reach the seat back ahead to pull himself up. When he twisted awkwardly and used his left arm to rise, his right hand fell to the carbon fiber shell of the prosthetic leg under his chinos.

"Sorry I'm so slow," Kevin forced a tepid smile when it hurt to move. "I'm not as spry as I used to be."

"Take your time, sir."

The train was swaying on an uneven section of track, so he couldn't kick off the steel spring in the arch of his right foot to bend his mechanical knee. Kevin O'Connor took halting steps behind the conductor, keeping his right leg straight and holding onto the seat backs.

"We don't make this stop very often anymore," the conductor said, when Kevin joined him on the platform. Farmland rolled by the open door, with a covered bridge across a creek in the distance. "What brings you to New Manor, anyway?"

"It's Alumni Weekend at Ethan North."

"Oh, I see. Well, we used to pick up cadets here at Thanksgiving and Christmas. But since Ethan North Academy closed, we haven't made this stop at all."

"Closed?" Kevin said as the train's brakes screeched and the car lurched. "That's news to me. But I've been out of circulation for a few months."

More like ... What? ... A year and a half? Kevin thought.

"Watch your step, sir."

Kevin held onto the handrails and went down the steps one at a time, leading with his artificial leg. He had to turn around and hold on with only his left arm to negotiate the final big step down to the gravel, being careful not to pull his unstable right shoulder out of the socket with his own weight.

He walked slowly into New Manor with his bag slung across his back, taking long strides with his left leg and letting momentum swing the mechanical leg forward. The town was as clean and orderly as ever, and the locals all waved and said hello. But past the Soldiers and Sailors Monument in the middle of town, the sidewalk became uneven, with tree roots pushing up under the concrete. Kevin had to work hard not to trip there, and he carefully planned each step to plant his heel and pull back on the mechanical knee with his thigh, to keep it locked as he walked uphill.

When he reached the low wall around the campus, he paused at the lower gate and leaned against the stones. Kevin O'Connor used to run across the campus, from the gate to his dorm room in Building '51 at the foot of Dynamite, but the path now looked impossibly steep.

There was not a soul in sight.

Is everybody in class? Kevin wondered. *Or is the old place really closed?*

He limped up between the chapel and the Gables, using his prosthesis like a pole-vaulter to climb the hill, and paused at the cannon. The leaves were turning with autumn's full glory when he entered Founders Hall by the side steps. The form of Colonel Hammond was unmistakable behind the president's desk. Kevin dropped his bag in the outer office and knocked alongside the open door.

"Cadet O'Connor reporting, sir."

Rocky Chambers jumped up and shook Kevin's hand first.

"Look what you see when you don't have a gun and it's out of season!"

Kevin pushed his prosthetic leg up to the desk and he strained to extend his right arm with his dysfunctional shoulder.

"Welcome home," the colonel reached across to take his hand. "It's good to see you, Kevin."

"I don't believe it!" Kevin said next, when he saw the third man in the office. "Is this really Walt Weiss?"

"KO!" Walter used Kevin's old nickname. "What happened to you, buddy?"

"Just a bit of bad luck," Kevin smiled and shrugged.

"We heard you were dead," Rocky laughed.

"Almost. I was a cop in Boston for sixteen years, but I made a rookie mistake on the Bomb Squad. A secondary device … well, anyway … enough of that. What's this about the school being closed?"

"You didn't know?"

"I guess I haven't been getting the alumni newsletters," Kevin smiled. "My ex-wife tosses away the chafe at our old address and only forwards the bills my way."

"Better sit down, pal," Rocky slid a chair up to the desk.

"Cadet Jonathan Chen walked into the woods on the last Sunday in May," Colonel Trip Hammond offered what had become a familiar refrain, "and was never seen again. The search for him lasted all summer and drew intense media attention. There was no way to reopen the school this year. I had to let the staff go."

"Old boy or new boy?"

"New boy. It was his first year with us."

"How old?"

"Sixteen," Colonel Hammond handed Kevin a picture. "A sophomore."

"No mystery there," Kevin shrugged, reviving his cop demeanor. "Some pedophile grabbed the poor kid."

"That is our worst fear."

"With good reason," Kevin set the picture back on the desk. "Slight build and a bright smile. He would have been irresistible to some perv cruising the back roads."

"Don't let his size fool you," Rocky piped up. "He was wiry! Jonathan Chen first came to my attention when he tied the school record on the physical fitness test, set by Red Saunders, way back in '59. He would have been tough to hold, I guarantee that!"

"Sports?"

"He only wanted to run your old event, Kevin." Rocky laughed. "Cross-country."

"Of course he was a runner," Kevin looked out the window. "Weren't we all, when we were young? But maybe he hopped into a car with someone anyway."

Walter Weiss had been quiet, but he spoke up to point something out.

"Hitchhiking has always been punishable by a General Order."

"Yeah," Kevin looked at Walter. "I know that thumbing a ride is one of the mortal sins. But if the kid wanted to visit a girl in Newport or Duncannon…"

His words were cut short by the rising drone of a motor, like a fast truck climbing the hill. But then the office windows shook with the rumble of a single-engine airplane making a low pass at the treetops. The throaty sound of the propeller seemed to pass a few scant feet over the roof of Founders Hall.

"Great!" Rocky looked at Kevin. "How long has it been since you've seen Derek Yeager?"

It was prearranged for Derek to land at Rocky's farm on the edge of town. So he and Kevin drove off in the teacher's old truck, a "Parsons County Cadillac," with a cracked windshield, a rusted bed, and snow tires on the rear axle all year long.

"Three on the tree," Kevin observed, when Rocky used the manual shifter on the column. "You don't see many of those nowadays."

"I don't plan on ever buying a new truck. If it works, don't fix it."

"So, why don't you still teach at Ethan North?"

"I was always a little too irreverent for the Holy Ground," Rocky shrugged as he steered the truck down a back road. "Okay, I was far too irreverent! I spent so many of my Army years in Japan and Europe that stories about *geishas* and *fräuleins* were bound to slip out now and then."

"I remember," Kevin laughed.

"It's better this way. I taught in the Parsons County schools until I decided that I was too old to work. Now I'm just a hanger-on around the campus. Luckily, Trip and I have managed to stay friends, although it was touch and go for a while."

The high-wing Cessna came in behind them with a roar, skimming a few feet over a field. It rose over a stand of trees and angled low over the truck before dropping a wing to slip down to the other side of the road. Then it rose up in a steep climbing turn and disappeared behind more trees.

"Neat!" Rocky exclaimed. "That kid can really fly!"

He ought to know, Kevin thought. *Rocky has owned a few airplanes himself, as well as every kind of motorcycle and sports car there is. What a life he's had.*

"Yeah," Kevin pulled up the cuff of his chinos to expose the titanium pipe above his shoe, where his ankle should have been. "I'm not sure I want to see him, Rocky. Not like this."

"What? Who cares about that? You guys were best friends."

"But I've never been good at keeping in touch," Kevin shrugged. "We talked on the phone a few times, years apart. But I haven't laid eyes on Derek since the day Trip kicked him out of school."

"So? You're both the kind of guys who live in the moment. Who has time for keeping in touch, anyway?"

"He never saw me when I was a Navy diver. Or when I was a hard-nosed cop busting heads on the back streets of Boston. I was really something, Rocky. I was in great shape. You would have been proud."

"I am proud. And I've seen old school chums reunite dozens of times. You'll see. It will be like the years never happened."

They arrived at Rocky's farm at the same time that Derek was landing on the edge of a hayfield, with big flaps hanging low behind the wings. The Cessna had a tail wheel and two large tires in front, all three of which settled gently onto the grass in one motion.

"KO!" Derek jumped down after the propeller stopped. "Kevin O'Connor, is that really you? No way!"

"Hi, Derek."

Derek was still lithe and full of energy, but his hair was longer and uncombed. And he apparently hadn't shaved in a few days.

"Get out!" he pushed Kevin's shoulders hard, the way they used to do, and Kevin stumbled backward and went down to the ground in a heap.

"Holy shit! KO," Derek reached down to help him up. "What happened to you?"

"I'm okay."

"No you're not."

"Hang on a bit," Kevin reorganized his limbs, then reached up. "I'll take that hand now."

"Sorry, pal."

"Don't be," Kevin said, standing again. "I'm fine."

Derek kept a hand on Kevin when he turned to Rocky.

"Great to see you, sir."

"Cut the sir crap, Derek. I'm not your teacher anymore," Rocky said, touching the cowling on the Cessna. "And this is a really nice ship!"

"It's not mine. I'm just bringing it down here for a friend, to be sold. But I sure wish I could keep it."

"Becky would love to see you," Rocky said, "but she's down in Harrisburg. We'll come back later. You're both staying with us, right?"

"I have a slightly different plan," Derek smiled.

"I can't wait to hear that! Anyway, Liu Chen and Trip are waiting in Founders Hall. Let's go!"

"Yup," Derek tossed his duffel into the truck's bed. "Let's get the big reunion over with."

Kevin struggled to get into the truck on his own, but he eventually made it. Derek sat between him and Rocky on the short drive back to the campus.

"KO, I can't get over it. You're a freaking mess, man!"

"Yeah. I am a freaking mess," Kevin nodded.

"Does your life suck now, or what?"

"Why do I feel better hearing you say that?" Kevin laughed.

"Because we're still best friends, and I'm being honest."

"Well, yeah. Some things suck, for sure. But I'm alive and breathing, so it's okay with me."

"So? What the hell happened to you?"

"So, I screwed up. But I was lucky. Usually, when you make a mistake on the Bomb Squad, you're dead for a long time."

"You always did like playing in the danger zone. Deep sea diving, guns, bombs … you were always even crazier than me, KO."

"Yeah. I guess it finally caught up with me."

"So why did they call you in on this missing kid? Couldn't the local cops handle it?"

"They didn't. I just decided it was time for a visit to the Holy Ground."

"This place was crawling with cops all summer," Rocky said. "State Police, the FBI, even some National Guard guys. It was crazy around here."

"I'll bet," Kevin said.

"No, I mean really crazy. Listen, our German Shepherd died that spring. Becky loved that dog! So it really pissed her off when the feds came to our farm and dug her dead dog up. But that's the kind of stuff they had to do, to try and find this kid."

"What do you think happened?" Derek wanted to know.

"He's two miles from the school at the bottom of the quarry or two thousand miles away in somebody's basement. Either way, he's dead as crap, after five months."

"That sucks."

"Man, I still have one good knockout left in me," Rocky raised a fist in the cab of the truck. "If I could only get my hands on whoever…"

"It wasn't Boomer," Derek spoke.

"You're probably right," Rocky agreed. "Boomer is a myth."

"No. I met him. Talked to him and visited his camp. You know that."

"I believe you, Derek. But I'm not sure that the person you saw was Boomer. It was probably just some old loner spending a year or two on Dynamite. Just a tramp, camping out. A hobo."

"He'd been up there for years," Derek insisted.

"Derek, the Boomer myth has been going on since before Trip and I were cadets, back in the fifties. The guy would have to be well over a hundred years old!"

"I saw him once," Kevin uttered. "By the incinerator, behind Building '51."

"You saw somebody," Rocky said. "I'll grant you that. But Boomer? I don't think so."

"I know what I saw," Derek mumbled, while Kevin shrugged.

"Now, you guys need to remember that the kid's mother is desperate. So don't go filling her head with false hope. There's no harm in going up on Dynamite and having a look around. But when you don't find anything … and you won't! Let it go."

"It's about time the damn place closed, anyway," Derek said. "Who needs Ethan North Academy?"

"I hate to hear you talk like that, Derek."

"Can you blame me? Expelled two weeks before graduation? Are you kidding?"

"Derek, you were wrong. You know it, and I know it."

"Trip was still an asshole."

"Put all that aside. We've got to find out what happened to this Chinese kid. It's the right thing to do."

"Why did you come back, anyway?" Kevin asked. "It doesn't sound like you're into saving the school."

"Actually … it was the mother's voice on the phone. Liu Chen. I think I want to meet her. Not that I can say why."

———

"Wait up guys," Kevin said, when they were climbing the steps to Founders Hall. "I want to see the look on Trip's face when Derek Yeager walks into his office."

Derek didn't exactly get welcomed home, like the others.

"Hello, Derek," Colonel Hammond said, from across his desk. "This is Liu Chen."

"A pleasure," Derek held her hand and looked into her eyes.

"Can you find this mountain man they call Boomer?" she asked.

"If he's still on the mountain, I might. No guarantees."

"And who is this?" Liu Chen turned to Kevin while Derek and Walter Weiss shook hands and became reacquainted.

"I'm Kevin O'Connor. Sorry for your loss, Miss Chen."

"I'm not giving Jonathan up as lost yet. Are you joining our search?"

"I don't think I'd be much help. I'm just here as Derek's old roommate."

"Are you kidding?" Derek spun away from Walter and rejoined the main group. "Kevin is definitely in on this."

"What are your qualifications?" Liu Chen asked.

"Kevin is a big city cop," Derek answered for his friend, "and a Navy diver. Plus, he knows the lay of the land around here as well as any of us. He's definitely in."

"You appear to be moving with some difficulty, Officer O'Connor."

"I'm not a cop anymore. I lost my leg in a bomb blast a while ago. But you should know—" Kevin pointed to his head, "—that a cop's brain is his best weapon."

"I see," Liu Chen nodded. "So this is your team, Colonel Hammond? A discredited oceanographer, a slayer of innocent animals, and a broken police officer?"

"Maybe we should all sit down, Miss Chen."

Trip Hammond continued after they all found seats around the president's desk, "These men traveled great distances to help you. We should welcome their efforts."

"Of course," Liu Chen nodded. "Forgive my impatience. There have been many disappointments. I'm sorry."

"Okay," Rocky leaned forward in his chair, "let's come up with a plan. Walter, how long will it take you to search the quarry?"

"One day, I expect. I borrowed a great sonar unit from the University of Rhode Island to map the bottom, better than anything the police used. If I see anything interesting, I'll dive down and take a look."

"Good. Derek, how about scouting Dynamite?"

"I'll do a little looking around up there. But if Boomer is still around, he'll have to come to me."

Liu Chen wasn't impressed.

"How do you hope to accomplish that?" she asked.

"I have my ways," Derek smiled. "You'll have to wait and see."

"What can I do?" Kevin asked.

"We turned my classroom in Eagle Hall into a temporary command center during the search," Colonel Hammond suggested. "Copies of most of the reports and research compiled by the FBI are still there. I'll unlock the files if you want to take a look."

"Sure," Kevin nodded. "I always did my best work on the streets. But I'll take a look the paperwork."

"Fine," Rocky sat back. "So we're agreed that we'll all work at least through the weekend on this?"

"I may not be much help," Colonel Hammond said, among nods of agreement. "This is Alumni Weekend. I'll have to spend time with any of the Old Guard who may show up. And there is a big meeting of the Alumni Association in the chapel on Saturday afternoon."

"You mean there's still an old boys' club?" Kevin asked. "Even with the school being closed, and all?"

"We have a small group of very dedicated alumni," the Colonel answered.

"But most guys really just don't give a crap," Derek scoffed. "Right?"

"Easy, Derek," Rocky said. "Ethan North Academy is in trouble, for sure. Now is the time for all of us to rally around. If all the alumni get involved, we might yet reopen this place."

"Well said, Rocky," Trip Hammond smiled. "So, where are you all staying? I could open up one or two of the faculty apartments for the weekend."

"I'll be camping in Building '51," Derek shrugged.

"I'd rather you all stay together in one of the faculty apartments."

"Boomer would never find me that way," Derek was sure. "I'll stay in the dorm."

"Our old room?" Kevin guessed. "What the heck. I'll stay there, too."

"I'll have to turn the heat on '51," Colonel Hammond was resigned. "That way you'll have hot water in the morning, too."

"In that case," Walter Weiss said, "I'll stay in '51, too."

"That was Jonathan's building," Liu Chen reflected, "on the edge of the forest on Dynamite."

"Great," Walter stood up. "My gear is in my car. I'll bring it up there."

"I don't think so," Derek said. "Boomer doesn't like cars, and there were never cars up there when cadets lived there. So maybe all cars should be parked down by the football field after we bring our stuff inside."

"In that case, I'll go into town and get some food before I park for the night, so we don't starve in the dorm."

"Jeez, I forgot about that," Kevin laughed. "Going to bed hungry! Remember? No food other than a secret candy bar or hidden bag of chips in the dorm. After supper, we just didn't eat."

"Well, I'm bringing some Pennsylvania Dutch Birch Beer," Walter laughed. "I always had a bottle or two on the windowsill, to stay cold."

"Right," Kevin said, "I remember that about you. But there's an awful lot I don't remember about this place. I might have to take a day just to walk around and get reacquainted with the Holy Ground."

"Well," Walter drawled out a thought, "that's not a bad idea. I've forgotten a lot, too. So to do this right, we should relive a typical day … follow the schedule of meals and classes and so forth, from reveille to taps."

"I like the idea of that experiment, Doctor Weiss," Kevin laughed. "I mean, really … after twenty years, what does any of us remember?"

"That's a great idea!" Rocky said.

"Fine," Colonel Hammond nodded. "I'll talk to Miss Clouser about opening the kitchen up for the whole weekend. We were going to serve lunch to the alumni on Saturday, anyway."

"Neat!" Rocky jumped up. "I'll go home and get my gear and stay there, too."

His three former students only stared at Rocky Chambers, until Derek spoke.

"That would be kind of weird, Rocky."

"What?"

"You're a *teacher*," Kevin said.

"Don't be ridiculous. You're all grown men now."

"No," Walter said. "They're right. It would be weird. We were always left mostly alone in the dorms."

"I used to walk through several times a day," Rocky noted.

"Yeah," Kevin said. "And we all stopped what we were doing the moment the doors from the stairway opened."

"For sure," Derek remembered. "We were different kids any time a teacher was around. You guys wore green Army uniforms, and we were in cadet gray. I guarantee you that every cadet went on high alert whenever green was spotted, even all the way across the campus."

"Okay. You win. I'll go home to Becky and see you in the morning."

"That's something else I forgot," Kevin whispered to Derek as the group shuffled out of the office. "The first rule for cadets … don't snitch."

———

It was going to get cold that night. So when they met in the dayroom on the first floor of Building '51, Walter was wearing his old red and blue warm-up jacket with the Varsity "E" for tennis on the breast. Derek had on his well-worn Ethan North sweatshirt, with a Pennsylvania keystone and crossed rifles emblazoned on the chest, and Kevin went across the hall to the trunk room and found an abandoned red and blue jacket, which more or less fit him.

The men were speechless when Liu Chen walked in with an overnight bag. She was also wearing a cadet red and blue jacket, and they all knew that it was Jonathan's by the Varsity "E" for cross-country running.

"It's fine with me if she stays here," Derek finally said. "I spent four years in '51 dreaming about having a girl in my room."

"Right," Walter said. "So, is it agreed that we're all going to follow the cadet rules? No cigarettes, no alcohol, no roughhousing."

"All the fun stuff," Kevin muttered.

"How about hazing?" Liu Chen faced the three men and wanted to know.

"What?" Derek doubted. "Are you saying that your son was abused by the bigger boys?"

"Jonathan never said so. But you stated that the boys were always left mostly alone in the dorms. That sounds like the *Lord of the Flies* scenario to me."

"Yeah," Kevin said, "that sort of stuff just didn't happen. There were always practical jokes and some goofing around, but nothing really harmful."

"I agree," Walter nodded. "Remember, some of the kids living in Building '51 were as young as fourteen. The senior jocks just wouldn't allow one of them to be seriously mistreated."

"Plus, Trip would have kicked our butts if he ever got wind of it," Derek added.

"That's the way it was when we were cadets, Miss Chen," Walter said, "and nothing ever changes at Ethan North."

"I am reassured to hear this. And please, since we're going to be together all weekend, my friends call me Lulu."

"Great!" Kevin said, "let's go stake out some rooms."

"Go ahead and turn on the lights in most of the rooms," Derek suggested, when they went through the double doors at the top of the stairway. "If Boomer is out there, I want it to look like the cadets are back."

"Whatever," Walter shook his head disapprovingly, "but that Boomer stuff is nonsense."

"You are not a believer, Walter?" Liu Chen asked.

"I'm a scientist, Lulu. I can't take the measure of a myth."

"So you never saw him on the edge of the forest like so many other boys?"

"Walt wasn't interested," Derek answered for him. "We had to look long and hard to see Boomer."

"This was Jonathan's room," she said, when they had walked half-way down the hall. There were still the remnants of yellow crime scene tape on the doorframe.

"This was my room, too," Walter nodded.

"Then will you do me the pleasure of staying in this room with me tonight?"

"I hadn't expected that," Walt hesitated.

"Doctor, the campus is dark and deserted, and the forest is nearby. And I noticed that there are no locks on the exterior doors of Building '51, nor on the room doors. And you are a married man who is accustomed to sharing mixed-gender accommodations on research vessels, are you not?"

"Sure. I'll stay with you, Lulu."

"Damn it," Derek laughed, when he and Kevin left them and walked down the hall. "Another dream shattered."

"Like you would stand a chance with an artsy-fartsy grant writer from Georgetown," Kevin shrugged. "What did she call you? A slayer of innocent creatures?"

"Ha! You're a broken policeman."

"Can't argue with that," Kevin shrugged as he pushed his artificial leg down the hall.

"It's been a long time," Derek uttered when he opened the door to their old room.

"It's a lot smaller than I remembered," Kevin laughed.

The room held two bunks, an open locker with cubby shelves and two hanging racks, and a desk with two chairs. The unadorned window looked over the forest, across fifty feet of lawn.

"Look at this!" Kevin examined the back of the door near the knob. "The hole where we used to stick a nail into the latch is still here."

"Ha! Just to slow Rocky and Trip down when we were up to mischief after taps."

The men naturally put their gear on their sides of the locker and went to their former bunks.

"Remember this?" Derek said when he short-sheeted his own bed under a wool blanket.

"Yeah," Kevin laughed. "Making the beds in the morning was a pain. I never slept under the sheets, just under a blanket on top."

"Well, here we are again," Derek said when he lay on his bunk, fully clothed.

Kevin settled awkwardly into a chair at their old study table.

"This is weird. Fun, but weird."

"We haven't changed at all, have we?"

"No. Well, other than being a fat old cripple with one leg, that is. Inside, I'm still the same teenage kid."

"Me too," Derek said, standing up, "and it's time to begin another spirit mission!"

"Uh-oh, what are you up to?"

"Remember this?" Derek opened the window and leaned out into the cool night. "This is great! Walt is keeping a bottle of Birch Beer cold on his windowsill. Some things never change!"

"You're not..."

"Oh yes, I am," Derek laughed. Leaning out the window, he reached up and grabbed the heavy rain gutter on the eave above and swung himself outside.

"You might feel like a kid," Kevin warned as Derek caught the tiny ledge of bricks with his toes, "but your bones are going to break like an old man's."

"Did I ever fall?" Derek asked as he inched his way along the side of the second story. The course of out-turned bricks was only one inch wide, so most of his weight was hanging from the gutter. At Walt's room, he peered secretly around the edge of the window frame.

"They're talking," he whispered back to Kevin.

"Just steal the soda, Derek."

"No. This is great. They're sitting close, having a real heart to heart."

"Just take the soda bottle, you damned peeping Tom."

"Okay," Derek held on with one hand and reached down. He tossed the Birch Beer underhand to Kevin, who leaned out the window to catch it.

"God!" Derek laughed, when his feet were back on the floor in their room. "I'd forgotten how much fun that was!"

"Now what?" Kevin rubbed his right shoulder, which ached from reaching to catch the bottle of soda.

"Don't you remember? Rob from the rich, give to the poor."

They went quietly down the hallway and down the narrow stairs at the back of the building. Kevin took the steps one at a time, leading with his mechanical leg. Then he gave Derek a boost so he could reach up to disarm the fire alarm bell on the outside door with a wad of toilet paper.

"While you're down there," Derek joked, when his elevated position put him waist-high in front of Kevin.

"Asswipe," Kevin muttered.

When they pushed on the panic bar to open the door, the bell clatter of the bell clapper was barely audible.

"What do you think of that?" Kevin asked as they walked across the dark lawn at the edge of the forest. He stumbled, fell, and landed hard on his prosthetic knee.

"I'm okay," Kevin said after he rolled onto his side and tried to stand back up.

"What do I think of what?" Derek asked as he helped Kevin get upright.

"You know. What if someone took everything from Jonathan to touch his body?"

"It makes me sick."

"Yeah."

They stood at the concrete block incinerator behind the dorm and looked back at the lights. Walter Weiss was in the bathroom taking a piss and Liu Chen was standing at the mirror in their room, combing her long black hair.

Derek spoke the words in a low, controlled voice.

"I'll have to kill whoever did it, you know."

"That's crazy talk," Kevin looked at his friend.

"Don't expect Lulu to do it. And there doesn't seem to be a man in her life."

"If the kid was molested, someone should kill the guy," Kevin said. "But you didn't even know Jonathan."

"He's one of our kid brothers, and you know it, even twenty years apart. If we find out someone did something to him … even if we can't prove it to the police … I'll do it myself."

Kevin shrugged and Derek put the bottle of Birch Beer on the flat rock at the edge of the forest behind the incinerator. When they went back into Building '51, Derek hung a towel out the window of their room as if to dry.

By then, it was time for taps, and Walter was cruising around the hallway turning out lights.

"What time is reveille, anyway?" Kevin asked when he passed their room.

"Six forty, I think," Walter tried to remember. "Then exercises on the quad at seven."

"You've got to be kidding," Derek said.

"You wanted to relive a day as a cadet, didn't you?"

Kevin had already pulled his pants off. He sat on his bunk with his mechanical right leg fully exposed.

"No offense," he said, "but I'm not going to make it down there and then back up to the dining hall in time for breakfast. Not on this thing."

"Then we'll modify the routine and do our workout on the sidewalk in front of '51. Or, you could just meet us in the dining hall."

"See you out front at seven."

"Who put him in charge of this operation, anyway?" Derek asked after Walter moved on.

"He was two years ahead of us," Kevin pushed the button to release the suction which held his leg in place, and stood it alongside his bunk. Then he peeled the silicone sleeve from his stump.

"Then it's like our sophomore year again."

"I guess so," Kevin shrugged.

Derek got up to turn out the ceiling light at the switch by the door. He looked out the window towards the forest for a long while before he crawled under a blanket.

"Hey KO," Derek said in the dark, "Jonathan was a sophomore, right?"

"That's what Trip said."

"And we're sort of reliving our sophomore year."

"Yeah."

"Man, this whole thing might get sort of weird."

"Remember, it's all about Jonathan, buddy."

———

Sometime later, the pain began shooting down Kevin's leg which wasn't there. The pain came in high-voltage waves as he lay in his bunk. The demons swirled in the memory of his heel and seemed to bend the arch of his missing foot into a horrible cramp until the toes would have been pulled back to touch the heel.

With half the lower body weight, he had a hard time sitting up in bed. Kevin was sitting on the edge of the bunk, pondering the impossible distance to the locker on one leg, when Derek spoke across the dark room.

"You okay over there?"

"Uh … I guess. But walking from the train might have been too much. I'm having some wicked pains."

"You mean, phantom pains? In your leg that's not there?"

"Yeah, man. But the pain is real. It's the leg that's the phantom. Would you mind getting me the three pill bottles in my bag?"

"No sweat," Derek stood up and took the four steps to the locker.

Kevin heard the pill bottles rattle. Then Derek found something else.

"Hey, what's this?"

"Once a cop, always a cop. Did you think I was going to leave my gun home?"

"Glock?"

"Yeah, .40 caliber."

"Nice."

"I figured you'd appreciate it."

"Oh, I do," Derek handed Kevin the pill bottles, and he began twisting the caps off and swallowing the drugs.

"That's crazy," Derek laughed. "I've heard of pain in a missing limb, but I never thought…"

"Yeah, it was okay at first because I could lie in the hospital and imagine that I still had my leg. Now it just sucks."

"What are you taking?"

"Dilated. Gabapentin. Vicodin."

"Whoa. That's potent stuff."

"I don't take it often. Only when the pain is too much to sleep. Good night, Derek."

"I guess."

For a few minutes, nothing was said. It seemed that they both might sleep. Until Kevin spoke.

"Okay, about what you were saying? If we find who did this, let me pull the trigger."

"What?"

"Exactly," Kevin said. "What have I got to lose?"

"Just try and get some sleep, KO."

CHAPTER 3

THE BELL TOWER

"It kind of sucks to look at this stump every morning," Kevin said, sitting on the edge of his bunk the next day. "But once I get my rig on, it's not so bad."

"You look horrible, pal. How many of those pills did you take?"

"Enough to help the pain. And thanks for noticing. How about you?"

"These bunks are too soft. But that's the first time in years that I've had nine hours of sleep like we used to get."

Rocky Chambers was waiting for them in front of the dorm with an electric golf cart.

"I don't need that," Kevin protested.

"You'll never keep to the schedule without it. Remember, you used to run across the campus to make classes."

Then Walter lined them up on the sidewalk. They had on red and blue jackets, except for Derek in his Ethan North sweatshirt.

"Okay, by the numbers now," Walter said, and led them through the familiar sets of jumping jacks and squats and stretches.

"I'll tell you one thing that's coming back to me," Derek groused. "I'd forgotten how much I hated doing these dumb exercises outside every morning."

"At least it's not freezing today," Kevin laughed. "Shut up and suck in some of that clean mountain air."

Kevin kept up in the golf cart when they walked to the dining room in Founders Hall. All the tables were covered with white cloths, but only one held pitchers of milk and juice. Soon pancakes, a slice of Canadian bacon and toast emerged from the kitchen.

Colonel Hammond sat at the head of the table, flanked by Rocky and Walter. They all sat still and silent while he said grace. Then they dug in.

"Dibs on the pancakes," Derek reached.

"On you with the bacon," Kevin said.

"I'm vegan," Lulu said, when she waved off the milk and bacon.

"Really?" Kevin's interest perked. "How about Jonathan?"

"He is vegan as well. Absolutely."

The rest of the group stopped passing food and cast questioning looks at each other.

"We all ate whatever they put out," Derek shrugged. "Even the stuff we didn't like. It was plain but good. And there was always just enough. We never sent anything back."

"The kitchen should make allowances," Liu Chen insisted.

"My family kept kosher at home," Walter offered. "But when I was here, I ate whatever the other kids ate."

"None of us wanted to be special," Kevin explained. "We all just got along."

"Well," Lulu insisted, "I've always taught my son to be very particular about what he eats."

"Okay," Walter said, consulting the clock above the mantle. "We have about thirty-seven minutes until chapel. Let's stack these plates and get moving."

They trotted back to Building '51 in a pack, with Kevin following in the cart.

"If you remember, we rotated through the cleaning duties each week," Walter said. "Halls, bathrooms, stairways. But today let's just do our rooms."

"Yeah," Kevin agreed. "And you might want to stay away from the bathrooms for a while, Lulu. Most of us used to squeeze in a quick shower between cleaning duties."

"I'll wait until you men are done," she nodded.

The three old cadets cleaned their rooms and stripped off their clothes. The shower was an open gang arrangement with green tiles and four spouts. Kevin brought a chair into the shower room, so he could sit and take off his artificial leg, which he stood in the corner. He was holding onto the pipes and standing under a stream of water on one foot when Derek laughed at him.

"KO, you're a sorry sack of crap now, buddy. Why don't you just shoot yourself and get it over with?"

"In case you haven't noticed, gravity and your Alaskan diet haven't been good to you either, loser."

"I didn't realize how extensive your injuries really were," Walter said. "You've had a lot of surgery, haven't you?"

"I can't remember how many. They even took one of my abdominal muscles to try and save my leg, so I have a five-pack now."

"What a loser!" Derek laughed.

"I admire you, Kevin," Walter said. "You're handling it very well."

"Not like I have a choice, Walt. What else can I do?"

Derek detected that Liu Chen was waiting outside the shower.

"Hey, come on in, Lulu," he said, leaning out. "The water is fine."

"I'll wait until you gentlemen are done, thank you."

"Suit yourself," his smile was mischievous. "There won't be any hot water left."

"Four shower heads don't seem adequate for thirty boys," she noted.

"We were always in a big rush. Step out, soap, come back and rinse when someone else got out of the way."

Derek and Walter finished their showers and toweled off.

"Would you avert your eyes, Kevin?" Liu Chen asked as she stepped into the shower room after they departed.

"Yeah," he turned away and sat in the chair to put on his leg.

"Your friends are harsh. I'm sorry."

"No, they're my friends. I love it when they bust my chops, like back in the day. Sorry is the last thing I want."

"You were injured as a police officer?"

"The Bomb Squad. I blame this place," he laughed. "They're good at instilling an overdeveloped sense of duty and adventure in young boys. *God, Family, Country.* They drummed that into us."

"Do you love this school?"

"Actually, I'd forgotten all about Ethan North," Kevin said as he wrapped a towel around his waist and stepped out of the tiled enclosure. "It's coming back to me now."

He noticed that she couldn't help but steal a glance at his artificial leg.

"What about Derek?" she said over her shoulder. "He bears a strong resentment for the school. Especially Colonel Hammond."

"You'll have to talk to him about that," Kevin muttered. "But you may have noticed that Ethan North is sort of trapped in time. Cadet life hasn't changed much since the Spanish-American War, when the school and all of our silly traditions were founded. And even though he claims to hate this place, Derek Yeager is more like Teddy Roosevelt and the Rough Riders than anyone else I know."

———

Rocky was waiting for Kevin, Derek and Walter when they went down and stood by the cannon. They stood at attention while Colonel Hammond raised the flag.

"You're supposed to freeze in your tracks and salute the colors," Walter told Lulu after she jogged into the group while the flag was going up.

"Sorry."

"That's okay," Kevin shrugged. "Life is easy here, once you learn the rules."

"To help you learn," Derek mumbled, "you'd get a Special Order for that."

"What is a Special Order?" Lulu asked as they walked to the chapel.

"That's the bad boy list," Walter said. "General Orders are worse."

"So what would happen to a cadet?"

"For a Special, you wouldn't get promoted for a while. For a GO, you'd get demoted."

"That's all?"

"You'd lose some privileges, too." Kevin offered. "But rank was how we kept score."

They went into the chapel and sat in the pews under the high ceiling. Colonel Hammond stood in front of them, before the stage and pulpit.

"So," Derek folded his arms across his chest, "are you going to say a few inspirational words, Colonel? *Winners never quit, quitters never win?*"

"*Look like a champion, act like a champion, be a champion,*" Kevin offered.

"I'm happy that you remember those pearls," Colonel Hammond smiled.

"How about the school song?" Walter laughed. The others joined him in the first verse.

"*Mid the hills of Pennsylvania stands the school we love, our devotion is as steadfast as the stars above...*"

"You're off key, Derek."

"So sue me."

"Fine," Rocky stood, "now that you're all pumped up about your alma mater, let's get to work."

Eagle Hall was a modern brick dormitory in the Federal style. Colonel Hammond's English classroom was on the first floor. Some folding tables had been set up near the windows across the back of the room, but the group settled into the remaining student chairs with side writing surfaces.

"So," Walter asked, "where do we start?"

"The FBI generated a pile of paperwork," Rocky said. "Interviews, search reports and profiles. They're on the tables back there."

"Who are the suspects?" Kevin wanted to know.

"There were several persons of interest," Colonel Hammond offered. "Primarily, a bachelor farmer named Bruce Martin. He's lived on the family farm with his hired hand since his parents died."

"The big farm down by the ice pond?" Derek asked. "That old guy was a jerk. He used to flip out if we took a shortcut across his hayfields."

"That guy was pretty weird," Kevin scratched his chin, "and isn't his handyman kind of ... different?"

"Adolph has a lazy eye and a club foot," Rocky shrugged. "He's lived with Bruce Martin for decades. Most of the locals don't want to think about their relationship. Whatever it is."

"How about Boomer?" Derek asked. "Did the feds find any trace of him on Dynamite?"

"Only some old campsites," Colonel Hammond said. "And there was no way to attribute them to a mysterious mountain man."

"I'm still leaning towards some stranger from outside of Parsons County," Kevin shrugged. "Maybe from another state."

"Out of state license plates would not go unnoticed around here," Rocky stood up and went to the chalkboard. "Parsons County has fifteen covered bridges, twenty-four churches, and not one traffic light. So let's take another look."

He drew a big cross of chalk along the lines of the main roads, with the Soldiers and Sailors Monument at the center of New Manor.

"Up here in the northwest corner, we have Ethan North Academy and the covered bridge on the other side of Dynamite Mountain. The quarry and the Little Juniata River are to the northeast. To the southeast, the fossil pits and Nob Hill Village. To the southwest, the ice pond and the Martin farm. Jonathan could have been headed to any of these places that afternoon."

"What are these fossil pits you mentioned?" Liu Chen asked.

"They're a popular hiking destination for cadets," Walter Weiss offered. "You can easily pick small fossilized fish skeletons and shells out of the bank. The sandstone dates from the Silurian Period, I believe."

Derek excused himself and left the classroom, with a mischievous smile at Kevin.

"Did Jonathan often go hiking by himself?" Kevin asked.

"Not usually. Of course, in autumn, the old boys show the new boys the places to go, and the routes that avoid the main roads, and the rare unfriendly farmer like Martin. The new boys usually head out on their own in the spring months."

"The FBI did make note of something which happened when Jonathan was hiking with a friend, the week before," the colonel pointed out.

"Oh?" Kevin's interest was piqued.

"It was probably nothing," Rocky said. "He went over Dynamite to the covered bridge with another cadet. On the way back, some hillbilly kids came out on their front porch and made fun of his Asian features."

"Unfortunately," Walter shrugged, "I suppose there are always some of them around."

"Not many. Anyway, when Jonathan tried to talk to the kids, the father came out and told Jonathan and his pal to keep moving. That his kind—and I'm sure he was referring to Jonathan's brown skin— weren't welcome around there."

"I'd like to talk to those people," Liu Chen sighed. "But the FBI would not tell me which house."

"I know the house," Rocky said. "It's got distinctive colors. The paint was stolen from the railroad. Of course, the place is falling down since it was last painted thirty years ago."

"Jonathan had told friends he was going to the fossil pits the day he disappeared," Colonel Hammond said. "But he was last seen heading up Dynamite. So the FBI theorized that he was actually going back to confront those kids."

"My son is a very headstrong young man," Liu Chen sighed.

That was when the bells began. They chimed out the quarter hour in four notes, like London's Big Ben, sending the melody reverberating across the campus.

"That's what has been missing!" Kevin suddenly realized. "The bell tower!"

"Yes," Walter nodded. "The bells! It's good to hear them again!"

Rocky started to stand, but the colonel waved him down.

"Let me nip this in the bud," Trip Hammond said.

———

Derek Yeager was sitting in one of the stone arches atop the bell tower, with a foot dangling from the ledge, when Colonel Hammond came up the steep stairs to stand between the large bronze bells.

"You're still the prankster, aren't you, Mister Yeager?"

"We need the bells," Derek shrugged. "It didn't feel like Ethan North Academy without them."

"I turned the bells off on the day that the last cadet left the campus," Colonel Hammond said. "I silenced them until our students return to us."

"We're back," Derek's grin was overtly facetious.

"You should have asked before you turned the timer back on."

"I had my reasons, Trip."

"You've been waiting a long time to call me by my nickname, haven't you?"

"Twenty years, buddy."

"Derek, I am still the president of this institution. I am personally responsible and accountable to the board of directors. So I must insist that while you are on my campus, you behave like the gentleman of honor we always hoped you would become."

"Big words, Trip. The last time I heard words like that was when you expelled me, two weeks before graduation."

Colonel Arthur C. W. Hammond III looked away from Derek. His gaze wandered across the panorama of the campus and the town below.

"It's time for drill period," he finally said and turned to go down the ladder into the tower. "And you should have shaved this morning, Mister Yeager."

"Stop telling me how to live my life, Trip!"

———

"Not for me, thanks," Lulu said when they went upstairs in Building '51 and retrieved their rifles from the racks in the gun room.

"Take one," Walter said. "It's drill period. You want to live a complete day as a cadet, don't you?"

"I never approved of Jonathan being exposed to guns," she frowned.

"Did you ever actually hold a real firearm?" Derek asked. "Just take one, and do what we do."

"I don't know … is this loaded?"

"That's the first thing you do," Derek held the rifle at high-port arms and snapped the bolt back with his left thumb. "Look in your chamber and make sure it is clear."

"Relax, Lulu," Walter said. "The firing pins have all been removed. But learning safe gun handling habits is important." He gently pushed the barrel of her rifle away from his face. "Like keeping the muzzle pointed in a safe direction."

"What kind of gun is this?"

"You are holding an M-1 Garand," Kevin said. "An eight-round, clip-fed, gas-operated, semiautomatic, shoulder-fired weapon. Standard issue, in World War II and Korea."

"Arguably the greatest infantry weapon of all time," Derek softly said, admiring the Garand rifle in his own hands.

"Did you shoot these?"

"No. There is a .22 rifle range in the basement of Eagle Hall for cadets who want to shoot. But each of us was issued an M-1 to care for. Keeping it clean and safe was a point of pride."

"Lulu," Walter said, "Ethan North wouldn't be a real military academy without real rifles."

"Careful of your thumb," Derek coached her, when she pushed down on the follower. "The spring closes the bolt with authority."

"M-1 thumb!" Walter laughed. "The cadet injury of shame!"

Rocky and Trip were waiting for them on the sidewalk in front of the dorm. They naturally fell into a line, with the butts of their rifles next to their right feet.

"Carry on, Mister Weiss," the Colonel said, and Walter stepped in front of the squad. He led them through the manual of arms. "Right shoulder, arms! Order, arms! Port, arms! Left shoulder, arms!"

The old cadets handled the rifles with precision, even though Kevin's deteriorated right shoulder took some of the snap out of his drill. Derek slapped his with the hardest hand, which made the forestock rattle, but Lulu was afraid to move her rifle.

"Show that weapon who is boss, Miss Chen," Walter said. "Treat it with respect and a firm hand."

"I don't think I can."

"That's okay," Kevin said. "It takes time. But once you learn it, you never forget it."

"Stack, arms!" Walter said, and they stepped together and connected their rifles like the poles of a tepee.

"I don't suppose you have a lesson plan prepared," Rocky asked, "do you, Mister Weiss?"

"No. But I could probably give one of the first aid or hygiene lectures from memory."

"I'm sure. In that case, let's get lunch."

"Yes, sir!"

When they unstacked their rifles and went into Building '51 to put them away, Walter stayed behind for a word with Colonel Hammond.

"I just remembered something, Colonel. I learned more about teaching as a cadet here, using your simple system at drill period, than I did all through my university education."

"Music to my ears, Doctor Weiss."

———

The bell tower chimed twelve times as they entered Founders Hall. Friday lunch was always grilled cheese sandwiches and tater-tots, with ice water to drink.

They decided to split up that afternoon. Rocky and Walter would reconnoiter the quarry in advance of Saturday's underwater search while Derek and Lulu would scour Dynamite Mountain for any signs of Boomer, in the places which only Derek knew. Colonel Hammond and Kevin would remain on the campus.

The route up Dynamite Mountain was a fairly well-maintained fire trail, cut into the forest behind Building '51 and the infirmary. Kevin followed Derek and Lulu to the edge of the forest in the golf cart.

"See you later, loser," Derek said as he stretched alongside the cart.

"Yeah. I forgot, which one of us usually got to the top of Dynamite first?"

"I won every time," Derek laughed.

"Like hell you did."

Lulu was nearby, bent over at the waist with her legs perfectly straight and her fingers wrapped around her toes. She wore Lycra running pants and a loose turquoise top. Her black hair was scrunched into a long ponytail.

"She's going to kick your ass, buddy."

"We'll see about that."

Derek wore his blue Ethan North sweatshirt and carried a small rucksack on his back.

"Let's go, Lulu."

They took off at any easy lope, side by side. The trail was not too steep until they got to the reservoir, a covered cistern above the campus.

"How far is it to the top?" Lulu asked, adjusting some sort of high-tech running computer on her wrist.

"Heck if I know," Derek grunted as the trail got steeper. "I never measured this bitch."

A few minutes later, they hopped over a small rock outcropping across the trail, and he stopped suddenly.

"Son of a gun," Derek muttered, looking into the canopy of trees. "I can't believe it's still there."

"What is it?" Lulu asked. "Boomer?"

"No. See that loop of rope around the branch on that tree?"

"Okay. What is it?"

"That's what's left of my old rope swing," Derek laughed. "I climbed that tree and put it up there ... what? ... Twenty-three years ago? We used to take giant swings over the ledge, way up in the air!"

"Where is the rest of the rope?"

"Doc Humbolt shot it down, years ago," Derek chuckled. "Tommy Greene didn't hold on tight enough, and he broke his arm and split his head open. The Doc hiked up here the next day in his tweed sport coat and bow tie, with his shotgun over his shoulder. It took him a whole box of shells to bring the rope down, but that was the end of my swing. But, boy! That thing was great fun while it lasted."

"I see. So, was that why you got expelled?"

"No. They never really pinned that caper on me. Doc Humbolt never even asked me if I put the swing up. He just chewed my butt, since it was the kind of thing I would do."

They took off running uphill at an easy pace again.

"How would you contact Boomer?" Lulu asked, not even slightly out of breath.

"I wouldn't," Derek huffed. "He'd just be sitting a few yards off this trail, and I'd stop and talk to him."

"Really? If it was that easy, why didn't everybody talk to Boomer?"

"They would never see him. Neither would you. He could be right over here, or there, and you'd never know it."

"Derek, are you sure that Boomer wasn't your imaginary friend?"

He stopped in his tracks and faced her.

"Do you really think I came all the way from Alaska to relive some childhood fantasy?"

"I'm paying for your services, Mister Yeager."

"You think I just want your money?"

"It has occurred to me."

"Well," Derek looked out at the forest. Leaves were falling, and he smiled at her. "I do want your money. But Boomer was here when I was a cadet, and I spoke to him, many times. Sort of."

"Sort of?"

"You have to understand, Boomer is deaf. He hasn't been around people much, so he can't speak very clearly."

"Did he at least tell you why he is living out here on the mountain, supposedly?"

"I never asked. According to the legend, he was a cadet at Ethan North at one time, who wasn't wanted by his family. So he ran up Dynamite and never came back down."

"That's ridiculous."

"It's just a kids' legend. But … consider the source. There are always a few Ethan North boys who feel a bit rejected."

"How is that, Derek?"

"Broken homes. Parents on overseas assignments. Teens who are hanging out with the wrong crowd. Boys from the meaner streets of Philadelphia or the Bronx. There are lots of reasons for parents to send their children to a place with structure and fresh air."

"What is it that you want to say, Mister Yeager?"

"Like maybe a single academic grant writer living in a trendy area, with a son and no man in her life?"

"You would do well to mind to your own business, Mister Yeager."

"Really? Would that woman be heartbroken by guilt for sending her teenage son off to Ethan North, perhaps to never be seen again?"

"Just do your job and find this Boomer."

"Don't you get it? Boomer was at least forty years old when I knew him. How many winters do you suppose he could spend on this mountain?"

"Find him, and I will ask him about Jonathan, in person."

"Good luck with that. He only mumbles about the things that he's interested in."

"And what would Boomer find interesting, out here in the forest?"

The vibrating peals of the bell tower ringing the half hour came up the hillside, reminding them that they were not far from Ethan North.

"Two things," Derek said. "I'll show you one of them, over here."

They had not ventured far off the trail and into the forest when Derek stopped and pointed at the ground.

"Try not to step on it. This is one of the oldest living things on Earth."

Lulu bent down and took a closer look at the vines.

"Blueberries?"

"No," Derek said, with a hint of reverence, "this is a box huckleberry plant."

"Explain, please."

"All this is one plant," Derek pointed to the low vines spread among the trees in the distance. "The box huckleberry reproduces by spreading roots and cloning itself. Individual trees and bushes come and go, but these same vines might have been clinging to this hillside for a thousand years. Maybe more."

"And why does some mountain man care about these scraggly vines?"

"I have no idea why. But, find the box huckleberry, and you just might see Boomer."

Lulu stood up. Then she turned and yelled, "Boomer! Boomer! Come out and talk to me!"

"I told you," Derek laughed as her words echoed down the hillside. "He's deaf."

She gave Derek an exasperated look and bent down to grasp a sprig of the plant.

"What do you think you're doing?"

"You may believe in folklore. I do not. I want to have this plant identified by an expert."

"I'm serious. That really is one of the oldest things on Earth. I wouldn't take it."

"You're not one to talk," she said as she broke off a few inches of vine. "You murder innocent animals for trophies."

"I have a covenant with the animals. You haven't spent enough time in the wilderness to understand it."

"I have a master's degree in electrical engineering, Mister Yeager," Liu Chen said as she tucked the sprig of vine into her collar. "Please don't tell me what I don't understand."

"Fine," Derek said, walking back to the trail. "Suit yourself."

When they reached the trail, they took off running uphill again.

"So," Lulu asked as they ran, "what is the other thing Boomer cares for?"

"I'll tell you later."

"Why not now?"

"You're too smart for me, Lulu."

They stopped at the clearing on the top of Dynamite long enough to look back at the town of New Manor and the Ethan North campus. The spire of the chapel, the roof of Founders Hall, and the crown of the bell tower were below them among the trees. Then Derek led Lulu down the path on the backside of the mountain, which took them to the abandoned farmhouse and down to the covered bridge across Sherman's Creek.

There was not much traffic on the back road. They walked into the shadows inside the bridge and examined the beams of the ancient structure. The sun shone through the gaps between the barn-board sheathing and illuminated the interior in pinstripes of light.

"Let's take a break down here," Derek suggested and led her to the grassy bank under the bridge. They sat against the stone underpinnings of the bridge, and he took two apples and bottles of water from his rucksack.

"There are two things I wish to tell you, Derek."

"Shoot."

"First, there is … was … a man in my life."

"Good for you," Derek bit into his apple.

"Secondly, Jonathan was very happy at Ethan North. He loved the school."

"Good for him."

When a car came by, the timbers of the roadway over their heads rattled and rang in succession like the keys of a giant xylophone.

"Now, what brought you to Ethan North, Mister Derek Yeager?"

"Things weren't so great at home," Derek shrugged.

"You were happier here?"

"I was. It was like growing up with one hundred and sixty equally screwed-up brothers, Lulu."

"That is exactly what Jonathan told me," she laid back on the grassy bank and ate her apple. "Except that he omitted the screwed-up part."

Kevin was heartbroken. Watching Derek and Lulu run on the trails which he loved only reminded him of all which he had lost, and he went back to the room in '51 and took some pills.

I'm useless, he thought. *What's the point of hanging on?*

He went to Eagle Hall to sift through the paperwork, without any expectation of accomplishing anything. But when he entered Trip Hammond's classroom, he was surprised to see a youngster sitting alone at one of the student desks.

"Mark Baker," the young man stood up and offered his hand, "Ethan North Class of '14."

"Kevin O'Connor, '94. Looks like you're getting an early start on your first Alumni Weekend?"

"I am, sir."

"Don't call me sir. We're both just old cadets, Mark," he waved at the papers and charts in the classroom. "I suppose you know what all this stuff is about."

"I do."

"You must have known Jonathan."

"I was in a different dorm, the Gables ... and a different class ... but the school is so small..."

Kevin sat down in the student chair next to him.

"What do you make of it, Mark?"

"It's pretty to think that Jonathan is still alive. And that he's not far away."

"Oh? How can you say that?"

"I feel it. Have they really searched everywhere?"

"Yes. Every inch of the campus, and all around New Manor. To-morrow, some of us are doing an underwater search of the quarry, once again."

"Every inch of the campus?"

"They've searched everywhere. Several times."

"But do they know all the places?"

"Maybe not like curious cadets know this place. But they were very thorough."

"How about the service tunnel? Jonathan might have wanted to explore down there."

"Which service tunnel is that?"

"The main heating boiler is in the Gables. You know that there are steam and water pipes which connect to the library and the gym? Also the junior school?"

"Yes," Kevin stood up and pointed at the chart of the campus on the wall. "Those are the oldest buildings. All the other buildings have their own more modern furnaces."

"Well, those pipes run through a tunnel. The furnace room is always locked tight, so few cadets even know it is there."

"I didn't know that," Kevin mused. "I've poked around every corner of this place. Even into the attic of the chapel, through the hatch in the ceiling of the offstage dressing rooms. But I never even knew there was a service tunnel underfoot."

"So have they searched the service tunnel?"

"I'm sure they did. They must have."

When Mark Baker stood up, Kevin saw that he was a lean young man of average height. His voice was soft, but his hard and determined eyes made him look older.

"I have to go down there to look myself."

"That's probably not a good idea, Mark."

Son of a bitch, Kevin thought, when he also stood up. *I can't stop him! Not on one leg, with only one good arm.*

"I'll be right back," the young man said.

"Wait up," Kevin heard himself say. "I'll come with you."

The entrance to the boiler room was outside behind the Gables, through a set of double doors at the bottom of a concrete stairway. Kevin gripped the iron pipe railing and made his way down one step at a time, keeping his mechanical leg straight.

"It's unlocked," Mark said as he held an old door open for Kevin to enter.

Oil tanks had been installed in the old coal bins under the Gables. There was a workshop in the basement, where the desks and chairs were repaired. Dozens of spare doors and windows were piled against the walls.

"The door to the tunnel is behind the furnace," Mark said. "It's always locked."

"Luckily, Mister Sweger's keys are right here," Kevin reached to a hook over the workbench.

"Have you ever been in here?" he asked as he waved cobwebs away and opened the padlock.

"Not in a long, long time," Mark mused.

"I suppose a year or two does seem like a long time at your age."

Mark Baker shrugged.

"It doesn't look like anybody has been in there in quite a while," Kevin said, peering into the dank recess. "Could they have missed this?"

"It's up to you, Kevin."

"We might as well go in a short way, as long as we're here," Kevin found a flashlight on the workbench and shined the beam into the tunnel. "Just to have a look."

"Let me go first."

"No," Kevin insisted. "I always go first."

"I know," Mark smiled.

Kevin went in, with Mark close behind. The passage was narrow and dank, with pipes on one side and a low arched ceiling of bricks. Mark had a hand on his back when they arrived at a division.

"That way to the library and gym," Mark said, pointing around Kevin down the main tunnel. "This little passage leads to the junior school."

A trickle of water came from the smaller passage.

"He could be alive in there," Mark said.

"He would have starved by now," Kevin offered.

"There is water. He could be so weak…"

"I don't know if I can crawl up there," Kevin doubted.

"Let me go," Mark insisted.

"Not on my watch," Kevin smiled as he worked his way into the cramped passage and crawled ahead on his hands and knees.

"What's that?" the young man named Mark asked, when a clanging noise rang through the tunnel.

"Steam," Kevin knew. "Someone must have fired up the boiler."

"Maybe you should get out of there."

"Just a bit further…"

When the pipe burst ahead of him, the side passage began to fill with steam. Kevin struggled to back out quickly as the vapor came towards him, pushing his artificial leg clumsily back. Then scalding water came down the tunnel like a river, just when he arrived at the larger passage and stood up.

"Get out of here!" Kevin pushed the younger man, but they both tripped and fell to the floor.

Kevin scrambled to get up, cursing his artificial leg, which had come loose. He struggled to slip the socket back onto his stump, but he couldn't get the suction to hold it in place. So he crawled out of the tunnel with the water and steam in hot pursuit, and his titanium and carbon fiber prosthesis flopping uselessly in his pants leg.

He was sitting on the floor of the furnace room putting his leg back in place when Trip Hammond came down the stairway from outside.

"What's going on down here?"

"I was searching the tunnel," Kevin said. "A steam pipe burst."

"Are you okay?"

"My hands and neck got scalded a bit," Kevin stood up, in obvious pain, "but I'll be fine. Where's the kid?"

"What kid was that?" the colonel asked.

"Mark. He was in there with me and got out first."

"Who?"

"Mark Baker. He graduated last year. Class of '14."

"Kevin," Colonel Hammond narrowed his brow, "there was no Mark Baker in last year's class."

———

Rocky and Walter drove to the quarry northeast of New Manor in Rocky's old pickup truck. They stood on the ramp where the trucks used to drive in, under a curving cliff of cut rock in the mountainside.

The site had been abandoned half a century earlier, and the bottom of the granite bowl had long ago filled with rainwater.

"We can launch from right here," Rocky offered. "My friend will loan us his outboard bass boat tomorrow."

"Good," Walter nodded. "It shouldn't take long to survey the bottom. This is a small area, and the sonar I brought from the university will show remarkable detail."

When they climbed back into his truck, Rocky had a suggestion.

"Want to take a trip to the Martin farm?"

"Sure," Walter quickly agreed.

They rumbled along back roads north of Dynamite, through the covered bridge, and found Bruce Martin and his hired man in the fields. They were loading pumpkins on a flat trailer behind a rusty Allis Chalmers tractor.

"Hi, Bruce," Rocky waved as they dismounted from his truck. "Same deal as last year, two small ones for a dollar?"

"I reckon so," the farmer eyed Walter with suspicion. He was a gaunt man, about the same age as Walter, wearing a flannel shirt over frayed long johns. He had on low-cut leather shoes, with no socks. His hired man was older, and he stooped and limped and did not make eye contact with Rocky or Walter when he put the pumpkins in the back of Rocky's truck.

"What do you think?" Rocky turned to his former student and asked as they drove away.

"Those are a couple of odd ducks. You say they live there alone?"

"Yes. Bruce inherited the farm when his parents passed away a few years ago. The hired man ... his name is Adolph Gretz ... has lived there most of his life."

"They look like real loners, Rocky."

"They don't go into town much, and I don't think they have many friends. I probably talk to Bruce as often as anyone, maybe just to say hello once a week or so."

"Do you think they had anything to do with Jonathan's disappearance?"

"I don't know," Rocky shrugged. "The FBI hasn't ruled them out, not by a long shot. They've combed every inch of that farm, which has become a real annoyance and embarrassment to Bruce."

They were headed back towards New Manor when Rocky asked if there was anything else Walter wanted to see.

"Actually," Walter smiled, "it has nothing to do with our mission. But I'd love to poke around at the fossil pits once again."

"Done deal," Rocky said, and he turned south at the Soldiers and Sailors Monument in the center of town.

The pits were actually a small slope of shale which had been exposed by a road-building project, less than a mile from New Manor. Rocky pulled his truck off the highway, and Walter began to pick through the detritus at the bottom of the slope. He found small fossils immediately.

"It's still amazing to me!" the scientist said, holding a nub of rock with a bit of skeleton etched on it. "This was a tiny fish on the bottom of the sea in the Silurian Period, over four hundred million years ago."

"I know," Rocky agreed. "It's hard to wrap my mind around that number."

"You know," Walter said as they climbed back into the truck, "that's the source of a lot of human misery."

"How is that, Doctor Weiss?"

"None of us can get past measuring time in human life spans. What's the point of our tombstones, which last what? A few hundred years? When that humble fish has been immortalized across the millennia?"

"I know exactly what you mean," Rocky nodded. "If we all realized how short our lives were, and how quickly we'll be forgotten, the world would be a different place."

"I prefer not to fear the immensity of the universe," Walter mused. "I like to embrace it. Maybe that's why we're here ... to appreciate all that grandeur ... and to try to understand it in a way which that fish never could."

"I need time to mull that over, *Herr Professor*," Rocky laughed. "Let's take the long way back to the campus."

They hadn't gone far from the fossil pit when Rocky turned onto a side road through rolling farmland.

"That looks like Doc Humbolt's car," he said, when they came to Nob Hill. "Want to stop and say hello?"

"You bet I do!" Walter said.

A long dirt drive led up the grassy hill to a parking area near the "village," which was a cluster of barns and workshops around three large whitewashed dwellings. Doc Humbolt and the hired man were standing alongside their cars at the bottom of the hill.

"Doc!" Walter grabbed his hand and pumped it enthusiastically. "You're still practicing?"

"Good Lord, no!" the doctor scoffed. "I quit medicine years ago. I just look after a few housebound neighbors, these days."

"You mean there are still a few Nobbers living here?"

"It's down to three old ladies," the handyman offered.

"Sister Sarah is going to die any day now," Doc Humbolt waved up the hill. "And Sister Beth won't be far behind. The three of them should be in a nursing home, but there's not much I can do about that."

"This has to be the dumbest religion … or sect … or cult or whatever it was," Rocky spat. "The men and women lived apart, because these idiots practiced total abstinence, even for married couples. I mean … no wonder they're nearly extinct … what did they expect?"

"Parsons County folks are live and let live," the handyman shrugged. "These ladies don't bother anybody."

The afternoon was cool and windless, and they all stopped and listened when the music of the bell tower echoed faintly over the hills.

"Time for supper," Rocky shrugged.

———

Friday dinner was fish sticks, mashed potato, and cut green beans.

"Doctor Weiss," Colonel Hammond asked, after saying grace, "are you ready to explore the quarry tomorrow?"

"We're all set. Rocky and I also visited the Martin Farm today and talked to Bruce and his hired man. I have to say, they're both downright creepy. They would have to be prime suspects."

"I reject the idea that any harm came to Jonathan on that farm," Lulu insisted. "Jonathan would have avoided such men by a wide margin."

"Well," Walter shrugged, "the highlight of my day was a side trip to the fossil pits. Finding ancient sea shells there when I was a cadet helped to spark my scientific curiosity. And it was great to see Doc Humbolt again, over at Nob Hill."

"Derek?" the colonel passed the green beans.

"We went up Dynamite and over to the covered bridge. Then around the mountain on the way back, along the Crogan's Gap road, so Lulu could meet the hillbilly family who taunted Jonathan."

"You spoke with them?"

"They stood on their porch and exchanged a few words with us down in the road," Lulu said. "My impression was that they are just exceptionally ignorant people. Considering the source, I don't believe that Jonathan would have been particularly troubled by any opinions they might have voiced."

"Don't judge Parsons County by those guys," Rocky muttered. "None of us has much use for them, living in that old shack on the public dole."

"The baby in dirty diapers told me all I needed to know about that family," Lulu shrugged.

"What did you see on Dynamite?" Colonel Hammond asked Derek.

"I'll look again tomorrow," the hunter shrugged.

"You can't hold on to the idea that Boomer's still alive," Walter scoffed, "and still living up there?"

"I don't know yet."

Kevin sat face down, looking somewhat dejectedly at his fish sticks and red hands.

"Kevin," Rocky said. "I hear that you had the most adventurous day of all."

"More of a misadventure, unfortunately."

"And totally unnecessary," Colonel Hammond frowned. "The service tunnel had already been thoroughly searched by the FBI. They sent a robot with a camera up the junior school branch, rather than risk an agent."

"Kevin just loves danger," Derek smiled. "Be careful, buddy. No more heroics, okay?"

"Yes, that goes for all of you," Colonel Hammond agreed. "Kevin, did you see anything interesting in the reports?"

"Just something I wish I hadn't seen at all," he looked at Rocky and Trip.

"Don't sweat it," Rocky said.

"Doctor Weiss," Lulu pulled the sprig of vine out of her pocket. "We did find one interesting thing on Dynamite. Perhaps you can identify this plant."

"I'm a physical oceanographer, not a marine biologist. This is way out of my wheelhouse."

"I was hoping that…"

"Not so fast," Walter smiled as he examined the vine. "I have seen this plant before. In Captain Horace's eighth-grade science class, we visited a colony near the Tuscarora State Forest."

"What do you mean by colony?"

"*Gaylussacia brachycera* is self-sterile and reproduces asexually. It lives in isolated colonies which are each a single biological unit, mostly in Appalachia. It reproduces clonally, by extending roots."

"So how old is this particular plant?"

"Age is determined by the rate of growth, so it depends on the size of the plant. One colony discovered very near here along the Little Juniata River in the nineteenth century was over a mile in length, so eight to thirteen thousand years old."

"You're kidding," Kevin laughed.

"Not at all. Some people say that the Quaking Aspens in Colorado are older. But box huckleberry is definitely one of the oldest living organisms in the biosphere."

Derek gave Lulu a silent smile. *Told you.*

"You say this came from up on Dynamite?"

"Sure did," Derek said. "But let's keep that our little secret. The fewer people who know that there is a box huckleberry up there, the better."

"Sometimes," Kevin chimed in, "obscurity is the best security."

"So," Lulu pointed at the sprig in Walter's hands, "how old is this particular plant?"

"That depends. How big is it?"

"Probably five hundred by three hundred yards," Derek guessed.

"Then this sprig probably grew from a seed deposited there as many as a thousand years ago," Walter smiled and handed the sprig back to Lulu. "Humbling to us humans, isn't it?"

"I'm pooped," Kevin said, when he excused himself after dinner. "That little episode in the tunnel kicked my butt."

Then he putted back to '51 in the golf cart.

Rocky Chambers also excused himself to go home to his wife for the night.

"We have about an hour before first study hall," Walter noted, when the rest of them were standing in front of Founders Hall. "Want to go into town?"

"Cadets are allowed to go into town?" Lulu asked, even as they began walking.

"For an hour after dinner. And on Sunday mornings, for church."

Walter, Derek, and Lulu walked down Carlisle Street to the Soldiers and Sailors Monument and the Parsons County Courthouse. They went into the luncheonette where cadets could buy French fries if they had some allowance money, and maybe meet some kids from town. Then they went across to the drug store, where the big excitement used to be the druggist putting on his auxiliary police hat and going out to direct traffic when the volunteer fire trucks were called out.

Derek said, "Let me get that for you," when Walter bought another bottle of Pennsylvania Dutch Birch Beer. Townies recognized Liu

Chen everywhere they went and said hello. One man leaned out of his pickup truck and asked if there was any news and offered, "If there's anything I can do."

"I've been living above Barton's store for three months," Lulu said as they walked back up Carlisle Street. "This town is so clean and nice. So well ordered. Jonathan should have been perfectly safe here."

"He was perfectly safe here," Derek muttered, "that's what's so frustrating."

They stepped back onto the campus through the lower gate, behind the chapel.

"I'm worried about Kevin," Walter said. "He's taking some very potent pain medications."

"That explains the episode in the utility tunnel," Liu Chen said. "And with his disability … should we keep him on our team?"

"Definitely," Derek had no doubts. "On his worst day, KO is the guy you want with you when the crap hits the fan."

"I always thought he was an invincible little brat," Walter chuckled. "Remember when we were skating on the ice pond and he fell in?"

"I know. He was acting like an idiot, as usual, going on the thin ice where none of us would follow. I don't know how he didn't freeze and drown that time."

"You saved him with some quick thinking, Derek. If Trip and Rocky had ever found out about that little escapade, the ice pond would have been off limits forever."

"Give me a minute," Derek said, when he parted with Walter and Lulu in the dayroom on the ground floor of '51. Then he went outside and behind the dorm to the incinerator. He used the back stairs when he went back into the dorm and went straight to his room.

"Hey," Kevin said from his bed when Derek came in. He was resting on top of the covers with his artificial leg propped against the wall.

"Hey, yourself," Derek said. "Slacker."

"Listen. I'm worried," Kevin uttered. "I found something I wish I never saw in those reports from the FBI, and I didn't want to tell you in front of the others. Rocky Chambers is a prime suspect."

"What? That's crazy talk."

"Not to the feds. He had access to the campus and no children of his own. Those are big strikes against him. That's why they searched his farm so closely."

"That's something, I guess."

Derek shook his head and went to the window. He took down the towel, folded it, and put it away.

"Huh?" Kevin said. "Why are you taking the signal down?"

"The bottle of Birch Beer we put out there is gone, buddy."

"You mean … Boomer?"

"Somebody," Derek shrugged. "Good night, Kevin."

CHAPTER 4

DYNAMITE

Saturday breakfast was a hard-boiled egg, oatmeal, and toast.

A cool gray sky seemed to teeter on the top of Dynamite and hang over New Manor Township down in the valley when they went outside after eating. Red and yellow leaves were falling and the morning air on the edge of the wilderness behind Building '51 was cool and pure.

"See you later, KO," Derek said, when he and Lulu set out to run up Dynamite once again. Derek had surprised them all by shaving off his beard and neatly combing his hair that morning, so he looked more like the rambunctious young cadet he had once been.

Kevin O'Connor's heart sank when he watched his friend and the woman lope up the trail and disappear into the forest for a second time.

I'll never charge up Dynamite again, he thought, taking a deep pull of the sweet air into his lungs. *But at least I'm still breathing.*

Across the campus, Walter and Rocky had loaded the dive gear and sonar unit into Rocky's truck. They were just climbing into the cab to drive over to the quarry when Kevin rolled over to them in the golf cart.

"Are you satisfied with that paperwork already?" Rocky asked him.

"Nope. But I don't want to stay behind, either. I'll go to the quarry with you guys."

"The boat we're using isn't very big," Walter offered, pointing to the bass boat with an outboard motor on a trailer behind Rocky's truck.

"I'll wait near the truck," Kevin said as he left the golf cart and climbed into the old pickup.

"I don't know whether I want to find Jonathan today or not," Walter mused as the three of them drove away from the campus.

"At least that would end it for Liu Chen," Rocky's jaw was set.

Not much else was said as they drove over to the east side of Dynamite. Walter put on his dry suit when they got to the quarry while Rocky backed his truck to the water and readied the boat for launching.

"Nice gear," Kevin said, when he stood and watched Walter load his dive gear and the sonar into the boat. "You never saw me when I was a Navy diver. I can't even swim now."

"Everybody can swim," Walter shrugged as he pulled up the zipper on his suit. "The human body wants to float."

"Yeah. But it's hard to stroke and kick with one leg, and an arm I can't lift over my head," Kevin shrugged. "Not to mention, if I fall in with this thing on—" he tapped his titanium leg "—it's taking me straight to the bottom."

"Then you better stand back from the edge," Walter smiled.

They launched the boat, and Rocky used the outboard motor to make a quick pass around the small lake in the quarry. Then he shut off the outboard and used the electric trolling motor while Walter streamed the sonar array off the stern and watched the screen to take readings on the bottom.

Kevin stood by the truck and watched them troll around the water for a while. Then he made his way to higher ground and a better view by limping up the ramp cut into the cliff face. He'd only gone a short way up the gravel slope when he found a flat rock to sit on.

The exertion of climbing the incline made his stump ache. Phantom pains electrified his right knee and ankle, neither of which was really there, with a million volts of pain. So Kevin found the pills in his pocket and swallowed them.

A few minutes later, a small voice from above startled him.

"Mister, are you okay?"

Kevin turned to see a young boy on the next higher tier of rock, ten feet over his head.

"I'm fine. Do you live around here?"

"Yes," he waved, "over there. Are they looking for that kid?"

"Yes," Kevin nodded.

"He's in there," the boy said. He looked to be twelve or thirteen years old, with red hair and freckles. "That's what everybody says."

"If he is, they'll find him."

"There's no bottom," the kid shrugged, like everybody knew that Jonathan would never be found. "Why aren't you down there?"

"I'm not much for boats anymore. What's your name?"

"Matthew."

"Yeah," Kevin eyed the newcomer, still reeling from meeting the young man who had led him into the service tunnel. "Matthew, do you go to Ethan North?"

"No, sir."

"Good. Then come down here, where I can talk to you."

"No, sir. It's not safe."

"Why not?"

"These rocks up here are loose."

"Just come around," Kevin gestured to the ramp. "And be careful."

"Okay. I'll try…"

Against Kevin's advice, the boy began to climb straight down to him, instead of going the easy way around. Small rocks fell down the cliff. He knew that he wouldn't be able to help the boy if he fell, so he talked to him to keep him calm.

"So, what grade are you in?"

"Seventh," the boy said, finding loose footholds over Kevin's head.

"Where do you go to school?"

"New Manor Academy."

"What? There is no New Manor Academy. It became…"

When the big rocks came down and pelted him, Kevin slipped and fell backward into the quarry.

———

"You should have dressed warmer," Derek told Lulu as they chugged up Dynamite. "We might be sitting for a long time."

"I'm okay."

Their strides came in unison as they ran side by side. Leaves were falling like colorful snowflakes and coating the ground under their feet.

"Isn't the box huckleberry over there?" Lulu asked when they were halfway to the top.

"Nope. A few hundred yards to go."

"I could swear…"

"See how deceiving these woods are?"

"Okay," Derek finally stopped and said. "This way."

They left the trail and walked into the woods. After a few minutes, they found the ancient vines.

"Let's walk all around it," Derek said. Then on the far side, he stopped and turned his back to Lulu.

"Would you grab that bottle of Birch Beer out of my pack?"

Derek put the bottle on a flat rock near the box huckleberry. Then they moved a hundred yards off and sat on the slope above the plant. Kevin took off his pack and sat on it.

"Now what?" Lulu wanted to know.

"Now we wait," Kevin said as he pulled on a wool knit cap.

"You didn't tell me we were going to sit on the ground. I didn't dress warmly enough for this."

"Then go back to '51. I can wait for Boomer alone."

"No thanks. I'll survive."

"Let's do like the natives," Kevin offered as he turned his back to her. "Sit with your back against mine."

"Will this really help?" Lulu turned and sat with her spine against his.

"A little. But you're losing most of your heat through your head and neck. And through your butt, into the ground. Next time, bring a hat or a hood, and something to sit on."

"There's going to be a next time?"

"I don't know. That's up to Boomer."

After a few minutes, she put her chin over her shoulder and spoke close to his ear, "Is Kevin O'Connor crazy?"

"It's just the pain medications."

"Are we crazy? Sitting here looking at some old plant?"

"I'm okay. I'm not so sure about you."

Wisps of fog came up the slope and lay low in the vines. They sat still and silent for an hour or more.

"I need to get some blood moving," Lulu finally stirred.

When she shifted her weight to get up, Derek reached around to hold her down.

"You're too tense. Relax."

"This is insane. We can't just sit here. Let's go look for him."

"Just sit. Try some of that ancient Chinese meditation stuff."

"We revere our ancestors. How would that help now?"

"What are you afraid of, Lulu?"

"If you must know," she sighed, "I'm afraid of what they might find in the quarry."

"I know."

"And I'm afraid that this might be some elaborate ruse to keep me distracted while that happens."

"It isn't. Sit still."

"No signal," Lulu muttered, when she pulled her cell phone from her fleece top to check the time. Then Derek felt her back stiffen against his.

"Something … someone … is moving around in there," she whispered.

"Relax."

A ragged figure leaning on a staff moved carefully through the box huckleberry plant. He wore a tattered wool blanket like a poncho, and he appeared to be mumbling to the vines.

"It's him!" she yelped. "Hey! Come over here!"

"I told you," Derek turned and held her down at his side, "he's deaf."

"Let's go to him."

"Just sit."

The bell tower sounded the half hour. The figure in the vines stood erect and turned towards Ethan North Academy when the first peals came up the slope. Then he raised his arms and swept his hands to the tempo of the bells as if he were conducting an orchestra.

"He hears the bells?" Lulu whispered.

"He does. That's the second thing he loves. The music of the bell tower."

"You said he was deaf!"

"He is."

"Then how..."

"I don't know. Maybe the range of his hearing is limited? Or maybe he senses the vibration among the trees? I don't know how."

When the tolling of the bells ended, he plucked his scraggly beard and leaned on his staff and turned directly towards them.

"He sees us!"

"He's seen us all along," Derek muttered. "Just relax."

The ancient one moved slowly towards them. Derek could feel Lulu's excitement when he found the bottle of Birch Beer and raised it, saluting Derek. Then he put the bottle into his bag and cautiously approached where they sat.

"Dera, is that you?"

"That's what he calls me," Derek whispered to her, "since he can't say sharp sounds like K. But he can read lips pretty good if he gets close enough."

Then he said, "Hi, Boomer," and waved.

"Ha ha," the man laughed and got closer, "you're old."

"I'm getting there," Derek smiled. "Boomer, this is Lulu."

"Lu-lu."

"Have you seen a lost boy?" Lulu eagerly asked. "Have you seen Jonathan?"

"No," he uttered, and turned back towards the vines, obviously not wanting to talk about any lost child.

"Boomer," Derek held Lulu tight at his side and asked, "what happened to your hand?"

"I cut it," he smiled and turned back to Derek.

"Who put that bandage on your hand?"

"Don't know," he shrugged. "Nice man."

"Okay," Derek held his hands open at his side. "Have you seen a boy from the school up here? A boy with black hair?"

Boomer looked away but nodded yes.

"Eyes," the old man pointed to Lulu, "like you."

"A boy with eyes like mine? Where?"

He waved across the mountain to the southeast.

"Where?" Lulu tried to stand up, but Derek held her down with an arm across her shoulders.

Boomer gestured across Dynamite to the southeast again.

"How far," Derek asked. "The river? The Little Juniata?"

"No."

"The fossil pits?"

"No. No."

"Then how far?"

"Hears bells."

"What? You hear the bells?"

"No, no. Eyes. He hears the bells."

"The boy with the eyes can hear the bells?" Derek was amazed. "He's that close?"

"Yes."

"Where?"

Boomer dropped to one knee and began to tend the box huckleberry vines.

"Have you seen him?" Derek asked again. "When?"

Boomer shrugged.

"Where, Boomer?" Derek insisted. "We need to find him."

Boomer shook his head no. Then he muttered, "Follow vines."

"Follow the vines? Follow the berries?"

He nodded yes.

"Show us," Lulu pleaded. "Please!"

"No. Go away," Boomer began to get agitated. "Men come!"

He swept his arms over the hillside like he was beating the underbrush.

"He's upset that the searchers disturbed the mountain," Derek whispered to Lulu. "And his vines."

"Winter is coming," Derek said to Boomer. "Come with us."

"No."

"You'll freeze," Lulu offered.

"No. Ma-tin barn."

"Martin's barn?" Derek guessed. "You stay in Bruce Martin's barn?"

"Snow … cold … Ma-tin barn."

"Is Jonathan there?" Lulu had to know.

"No. No," the ancient one began to move quickly away. He stopped and gestured southeast, "Hears bells."

Then he vanished into the forest.

"Let's chase him!" Lulu exclaimed.

"No," Derek was firm. "Let the old guy go. He told us all he knows."

They got up and ran down the hill.

"We must notify the authorities," Liu Chen said. "The investigators must interrogate him."

"No," Derek decided. "He told us all he knows."

"But how could he know? He hasn't seen him, but he knows he's somewhere over there? That Jonathan is close enough to hear the bell tower?"

"Yup."

"And follow the vines? What is all that about?"

"I don't know," Derek stopped running suddenly. "We have to figure that out."

"This is a matter for the police."

"Listen," Derek grabbed her shoulders. "Yesterday, I didn't believe we had any chance of finding Jonathan alive. But I think that Jonathan is very much alive. And nearby."

"Then we have to go back and drag that crazy old man down the mountain!"

"No. He doesn't know where. Not precisely."

"This is insane!"

"I don't understand it, but Boomer knows things. I don't know how or why. But he knows."

"When I first saw him in the vines," Lulu rued, "I almost believed that he was an apparition. A ghost or spirit. But he's just a crazy old man. Do you think he really stays in Martin's barn in the winter?"

"Yes. He can't live up here in the snow and cold. And, somebody bandaged his hand recently."

"Bruce Martin?"

"No. We need to talk to Doc Humbolt."

———

"Where the heck did he wander off to?"

When Walter and Rocky completed their search of the quarry and approached the ramp in the boat, Kevin O'Connor was nowhere in sight. Until Rocky sighted a shape lying prone on a rock ledge at the water's edge.

"Kevin!" Walter voiced their concern as Rocky nosed the boat up to the stone face of the quarry. "Kevin! Are you okay?"

"Yeah," Kevin raised his left arm as they approached, "just get me out of here."

Walter helped Kevin off the narrow outcropping of stone, and he flopped into the boat like a gaffed fish.

"What were you doing down there?" Walter asked Kevin as he helped him sit up.

"There was another kid," Kevin shrugged.

"What?"

"There was another kid. I can't believe it myself. But another kid just tried to kill me."

"Just take it easy," Rocky said as he motored over to the ramp and landed the boat. "Tell us what happened."

"I went up a bit for a better view, and this kid came along on the ledge above me. I guess he was about twelve or thirteen. Some rocks fell on me when he tried to climb down, and I lost my balance."

"How far did you fall?"

"Only about six or eight feet. But if I hadn't landed on that ledge, I would have drowned for sure."

"Where is the kid now?" Rocky looked around the quarry.

"I don't know."

"He didn't fall in, did he?" Walter asked.

"No. He must have taken off."

Rocky and Walter helped Kevin out of the boat. His artificial leg had come partially off, so they held him up as he pushed it back on and limped to the truck.

"Okay," Rocky said, "why don't you have a seat in the truck while Walter and I get the boat on the trailer."

"Listen, guys," Kevin said, pulling his leg back into place through his trousers. "There's something else. The kid told me that he was in the seventh grade … at New Manor Academy."

"You mean New Manor Middle School," Rocky corrected.

"No. He said New Manor Academy. I'm sure of it."

Rocky and Walter gave each other questioning looks.

"Kevin," Rocky leveled his gaze at his former student, "there hasn't been a New Manor Academy since 1898. Colonel Jacob North bought the school when he came home from the Spanish-American War. He renamed it after his son, who had fallen off the Juniata River railroad trestle … Ethan North."

"That's what the kid said. He had red hair and freckles, his name was Matthew, and he was in the seventh grade at New Manor Academy."

"Take it easy," Rocky said. "You got banged up pretty good."

"You think I'm crazy, don't you?"

"You've been through a lot," Walter said.

"You have no idea," Kevin muttered as he gulped a handful of pills.

———

"We talked to Boomer!"

Walter and Rocky were in the dayroom in Building '51 when Liu Chen and Derek Yeager came in off Dynamite.

"He's real!" she chirped. "He's a crazy old man, but he's real."

"You talked to him?" Rocky was amazed.

"We sure did," Kevin smiled. "How did you guys make out in the quarry?"

"I discovered a few old cars and refrigerators," Walter grinned. "But that was all. I'm happy to report that Jonathan did not fall in there."

"That's great," Derek nodded.

"I knew that," Lulu agreed, with a sigh which said that she hadn't been so sure.

"Listen, Derek," Rocky said. "You can tell us all about Boomer later. Right now, you need to talk to Kevin. He's in tough shape. He fell off a ledge while Walter and I were out on the boat, and got banged up pretty badly."

"How did he do that?"

"That's the tough part," Walter said. "There was another odd event at the quarry, at least in Kevin's mind. He thinks that a second kid tried to kill him, but we didn't see anything."

"Knucklehead," Derek muttered. "Where is he?"

"We put him up in your room a minute ago," Rocky said. "He wouldn't go to the emergency room in Carlisle with us."

"Okay," Derek turned to go upstairs, "I'll go up and talk to him."

Then he paused and turned back towards the group.

"How about Doc Humbolt?" Derek asked the room.

"Doc retired from practicing medicine years ago," Rocky shrugged. "But he still lives in town and checks in on people now and then."

"Actually," Walter perked up, "we saw him out at Nob Hill Village yesterday."

"Do you think he'd make a house call?" Derek asked.

"Maybe," Rocky shrugged. "His number is still in the phone book. I'll give him a call."

"Derek," Liu Chen followed him into the hall. Apart from the others, she whispered, "What about what Boomer told us? We have to go look for Jonathan. Follow the vines and within the sound of the bells. Remember?"

"Just give me a minute with Kevin. Then we'll go check it out."

"You really care about him, don't you?"

"Sure. Sometimes he's a stubborn idiot. But I realized something yesterday. He's my oldest friend in the world."

"Then go."

"Listen," he turned back to her. When he found her hand, he wasn't sure who had reached out first. Only that her hand was in his. "We're going to find Jonathan, Lulu. Hunters have a sixth sense which I can't explain. But I feel it now."

"Then go. I'll wait here."

She didn't resist when he pulled her head close and quickly kissed her forehead.

Derek bounded up the stairs. The dorm seemed eerily quiet. Unmade bunks and empty lockers. When he entered their old room, Kevin sat up on his bunk and smiled.

"I've figured this thing out," Kevin said. "Kids from town did something to Jonathan. They at least know something. That's why they want us to go away."

"That would be a hard secret to keep," Derek said as he pulled up a chair and sat backward on it, arms folded across the backrest, "don't you think?"

"Yeah," Kevin pulled his elbow in and flopped back down on his bunk. "But there has to be some explanation. A lot of weird stuff is going on around here."

"You dope," Derek Yeager laughed. "How did you survive for twenty years without me around to keep an eye on you?"

"It wasn't easy," Kevin shrugged, and looked at the artificial leg propped next to his bunk. "What happened, anyway? I always thought we'd keep in touch."

"Alaska is a long way from Boston."

"You think? Maybe we were just worried that we wouldn't like each other after we grew out of this place?"

"Could be. But you seem like a pretty stand-up guy to me. You're a regular freakin' hero in the City of Boston, the way I hear it."

"Yeah. Right."

Kevin and Derek searched each other's eyes and saw that they were the same as always.

"You want to know something, Derek? I'd never say this to anybody else. But sometimes ... I wish I had died in that blast."

"Oh? I ... don't like the sound of that. The Kevin I knew was no quitter."

"Oh my God," Kevin's face suddenly changed to a pained laugh. "Is Derek Yeager—of all people!—going to quote Ethan North platitudes to me? *Winners never quit, quitters never win.*"

"*You can if you think you can,*" Derek smiled.

Another voice startled Derek and Kevin.

"I'm surprised that you remember that philosophy for simpletons they used to feed you boys," Doctor Otis V. Humbolt said, standing in their doorway in his tweed jacket and bow tie, with a small leather medicine bag in his hand. "But then again, the softer the clay, the easier it is to mold."

"Doc!" Derek stood up. "Thanks for coming."

"How could I stay away," he commandeered the chair and sat next to Kevin, "when the two biggest boobs in the history of Ethan North Academy have returned? Now," the doctor said, hovering over Kevin, "what happened to you?"

"I had a close encounter with an improvised explosive device," Kevin uttered.

"Well, I can see that!" Doc Humbolt scoffed. "I mean these more recent cuts and scrapes."

"I took a tumble on a granite ledge over at the quarry."

"Hmm. Serves you right for going rock climbing with one leg," the doc pointed at his neck. "What about these burns?"

"That happened down in the service tunnel under the Gables. A steam pipe burst when I was in there looking for Jonathan."

"There's a tunnel under the Gables?" Doc Humbolt turned to Derek. "I didn't know that."

"Not many people do," Derek nodded. "So, what do you think about this guy?"

"My diagnosis is ... he's a damn wreck."

The doctor opened his bag and began cleaning and dressing Kevin's wounds.

"This is nothing new," Doc Humbolt said. "Both of you. How many times did you slip and fall when you were out running around these hills like a couple of idiots?"

"We were on the cross-country team," Kevin shrugged. "Everybody takes a tumble, now and then."

"No. It was more than that. I used to see you two when I was out making house calls, running like wild dogs in the rain and snow. I think you used to try to push and trip each other."

"It was all for fun," Derek shrugged.

"You had way too much energy, if you ask me," the doctor shrugged as he tweezed a pebble out of Kevin's elbow. "You two had to run every day, so you wouldn't explode."

"After being cooped up in a classroom all day," Kevin mused, "who wouldn't want to go out and run?"

"You probably miss that," Doc Humbolt looked directly in Kevin's eyes. "All that freedom to move and run."

"You're a smart man, doc," Kevin admitted.

"Well, you'll live," he closed his bag. "Now, what's this nonsense about boys trying to kill you?"

"I can't explain it, doc."

"I can. You're hallucinating. What drugs are you taking?"

Kevin showed him the pill bottles.

"You're taking these together? No wonder you're seeing things. Do you have children, Kevin?"

"I do. Two boys."

"How are they doing?"

"Okay, I guess ... I haven't seen them in a while. They live with their mother now. And her new husband."

"Well, isn't your problem obvious?"

"I guess you're right."

"Get off the drugs," the old doctor stood up, "and everything will get better."

"The pain is too bad, doc."

"Oh, no it's not! Stop feeling sorry for yourself! That's the problem, Kevin."

"I forgot about your famous bedside manner," Kevin laughed.

"After forty years of tending to Ethan North boys," the doctor smiled, "I've perfected it, don't you think?"

When Doctor Humbolt picked up his medicine bag and stepped to the door, Derek stopped him in his tracks.

"Hey, doc, speaking of your bedside manner, I saw Boomer today. There was a fresh bandage on his hand."

"Oh? So you talked to him?"

"So you do know him," Derek muttered. "Why didn't you tell me?"

"Why end a grand Ethan North myth?" Doc Humbolt wryly smiled. "Your cockamamie tales of the Mountain Man provided us all with endless hours of entertainment."

"Wait," Kevin sat up on his bunk, "you've both talked to Boomer?"

"Not often," Doctor Humbolt admitted, "and never on the mountain. He comes to Bruce Martin's barn now and then when he needs help. I suspect that he lives there in the winter months, too."

"This might sound like a dumb question," Kevin said, "but I've got to ask. Was this character an old Ethan North cadet?"

"Of course not," Doc Humbolt laughed. "And he wasn't deafened in a blast at the quarry, either. He's just some old hobo who came to town on the railroad, I imagine, and never left."

"So he is a suspect in Jonathan's disappearance," Kevin offered.

"I doubt it," the doctor shook his head. "I told the FBI that there was at least one hermit spending time up on Dynamite. But the weather was fine, and he was off on the mountain, where nobody could find him. So they just assumed that I was talking about this other John Doe, who wandered into the asylum at Harrisburg and died, the summer before last."

"Boomer ... or whatever his name is," Derek said, "told Liu Chen and me that Jonathan was somewhere southeast of town, and close enough to hear the bells. Follow the box huckleberry vines, is what he said."

"I don't know how he could know that. But if he spends his time wandering the forest, maybe he did see something."

"What's out that way?" Derek tried to remember.

"Off the highway? Not much. Just farmland and the fossil pits. And Nob Hill Village, of course."

"Then we're going to Nob Hill," Derek's jaw was set by then.

"Right now?" Doctor Humbolt looked surprised.

"You bet we are. All of us."

"They won't even talk to you," the doctor said. "I'd better come along."

"Great. Let's go."

"Wait for me," Kevin sat up again.

"I don't think so," doc laughed. "One look at you would scare the old betties out of their bloomers."

"Doc is right, Kevin. You should stay here."

"Okay. But grab my gun out of the locker and bring it over here, would you? I can't really hop over there on one leg if I need it."

"Hey, you're in '51," Derek shrugged. "The safest place on Earth. Why would you need your gun?"

"In case you haven't noticed, I'm helpless. I can't even fight off seventh graders. And if you all go, I'll be all alone here."

"Okay," Derek shrugged and found Kevin's .40 caliber Glock semiautomatic. "Be careful with this thing, buddy."

"I have my doubts about this," Doctor Humbolt offered. "Just remember, Kevin, any seventh graders who come in the door are probably hallucinations. But don't shoot them. They just might be real kids."

"Or one of us," Derek laughed. "See you in a bit, pal."

———

Derek and Liu Chen rode over to Nob Hill in Doctor Humbolt's Buick sedan. Rocky and Walter followed in Rocky's dilapidated old pickup truck.

"I was just going home for the night," the caretaker said when he met them in the parking area at the bottom of the hill.

"We need to talk to them," Doc Humbolt stated.

"Good luck," Leroy Jenks pulled the collar of his coat closed. "They're sitting down to supper."

"This is the missing boy's mother," Rocky offered.

"I know," Leroy touched his hat. "Evening, ma'am."

They were all looking at the caretaker, expecting an answer to their request.

"They might allow Doc Humbolt in," Leroy finally said. "And the mother."

"I would like for Derek to come, as well," Lulu insisted.

"They won't like him … hard-boiled men scare the sisters. No offense meant, friend."

"No sweat," Derek smiled. "That's a fact."

"Derek may be a little rough around the edges," Lulu said. "But he has good instincts. I need his advice."

"Okay," Leroy said. "I'll give you a ride up behind the tractor. But you better leave your cell phones and other gadgets in your car. The sisters don't allow anything electric in their house."

He got the John Deere out of the shed near the road. Derek and Lulu sat on the trailer with Doc Humbolt, and they chugged up the hill.

"Don't cars go up here?" Derek asked Leroy.

"Almost never. The sisters are still pissing and moaning about the FBI and the State Troopers barging in with a dozen cars and a crime-scene truck when they searched the place."

"Mister Leroy," Lulu asked, "in your estimation, how thorough was the search?"

"They were here all day," he shrugged. "The cops didn't like that the judge wouldn't let them bring any of their high-tech stuff into the dwellings. But they covered the woods pretty good. Some feds even shot a feral pig."

"There are feral pigs here?" Derek asked.

"There are a few around," he waved at the large pigsty. "With this many swine, some are bound to get loose."

"That's not good," Derek muttered.

"You're right about that. They're nasty critters. If they get you down to the ground, it's all over," Leroy Jenkins pulled the butt of a revolver out of his pocket for Derek to see. "That's why I always carry my little friend here."

"A wise precaution," Derek nodded.

"Three houses?" Lulu asked as they got near the village. "Does each sister get her own home?"

"Heck, no," Doc Humbolt chuckled. "There were nearly two hundred of them, at one time. The center house is the kitchen and dining room, with a worship hall upstairs. The house on the left was for men, and women on the right."

"Men and women lived separately? Even if they were married?"

"Married couples could sit together at meals and services. That was it."

"You mean…?"

"Yes. Total abstinence."

"How did they expect to survive?"

"Nobbers were pretty sure that they had all the answers, to everything," Doc Humbolt muttered. "They believed that if they lived chaste lives, the whole world would come beating on their doors, eventually."

"Looks like they were wrong about that," Derek said as the tractor and wagon arrived at the whitewashed clapboard house.

"If we get in, don't be alarmed by Sister Sarah's eyes," Doc Humbolt said as he knocked. "She's blind from cataracts."

"She couldn't have surgery?" Liu Chen asked.

"Sarah has never been off Nob Hill, supposedly. She hasn't even been out of the house in God knows how long."

No one came to the door in response to Doc Humbolt's knocking. But a woman eventually appeared at a window, wearing a bonnet and a plain, homespun dress. She appeared to be about sixty years old and wore no makeup. She looked at them and didn't say a word or lift an eyebrow or alter her countenance in any way.

"That's Diana," the doctor whispered as they moved to the window. "The youngest."

"Hello, Sister Diana," Doc Humbolt offered. "May we come in?"

"The boy is not here," the woman said, looking directly at Liu Chen through wavy panes of glass. Then she moved back into the shadows inside the big house.

"Well," Doc Humbolt turned to Liu Chen and Derek, "we're not going to talk to them tonight. Maybe tomorrow."

"That's unacceptable," Liu Chen demanded, and began banging on the door. "Open this door, damn it!"

"It's no use," Leroy Jenks said, still sitting high on the tractor seat. "Doc Humbolt is right. Maybe tomorrow."

By then, Liu Chen was back at the window and banging on the glass.

"Did you see how she looked at me?" Liu Chen exclaimed. "She recognized me as Jonathan's mother!"

"You're right," Derek said. "If they don't get television or newspapers, how would they even know that Jonathan was Asian?"

"I brought them one of the posters that were around town," Leroy shrugged. "And the FBI showed them pictures, even though they didn't want to look at them."

"No," Liu Chen insisted, "she looked at me and immediately recognized me as Jonathan's mother! We must get into this house!"

"Take it easy," Derek gently towed her back to the cart behind the tractor. "This is no time for a frontal assault. Let's drop back and think about it."

They were going down in the driveway in the cart when Doc Humbolt pulled out his mobile phone.

"Who are you calling?" Derek asked.

"Trooper Landon."

"Moose? Moose Landon is still the resident trooper in Parsons County?"

"Lucky for us, he is."

"Great," Derek muttered.

They didn't have to wait long for the State Police cruiser to pull up alongside their cars in the parking area at the foot of Nob Hill.

"That was quick," Doc Humbolt greeted the lawman.

"I was on patrol in this area," Moose Landon said, getting out of the cruiser and rising to his full height. "What can I do for you, folks?"

"I demand immediate entry to that house," Liu Chen pointed. "My son is in there."

"Hello, Miss Chen," Moose nodded and touched the wide brim of his trooper hat. "What makes you think that Jonathan is here?"

"A woman recognized me as Jonathan's mother. It was Sister Diana, I believe. She must have seen him, to make the connection."

"That's interesting," Moose rubbed his chin.

"And the mountain man they call Boomer told us that he was here," Liu Chen added.

"Whoa," Moose was taken aback. "You talked to someone up on Dynamite? A mountain man?"

"I bandaged his hand at Martin's barn last week," Doc Humbolt admitted. "He might have seen something amiss over here."

"Well, I don't know," Moose was torn. "That's hardly probable cause for a search warrant. And why would the Nobbers hold Jonathan, anyway? They've never had much use for children. That's why they're nearly extinct."

"He might be the first Asian boy they've ever seen," Rocky insisted. "Who knows what prophecy they might have imagined in him? I think he's in there, Moose."

"It seems to me that the mother has a legitimate concern here," the doctor stated.

"Doc … I don't know. The judge only allowed us and the FBI one day to search up here, with a lot of restrictions on how many troopers and agents could enter the dwelling, and what sort of equipment they could bring inside. It really amounted to a cursory examination, but he was worried about moving in on a religious community. Nobody wants another Waco or a Ruby Ridge scenario here."

"Come on, Moose," Rocky urged. "The magistrate will listen to you."

"Tomorrow is Sunday," Moose shrugged. "There's no way any magistrate is going to sign off a raid on a religious site on the Sabbath. Maybe Monday morning."

They heard the bell tower, way in the distance.

"Maybe we'll just knock the door down and have a look ourselves," Derek shrugged.

"Bad idea, Derek," Rocky said.

"We can't just sit here and do nothing." Derek was tensed and girded for action. "I say we take the damn place apart right now, plank by plank, until we find something."

"Derek?" Moose picked up on the name and focused on him. "I know you. Derek Yeager!"

"Guilty," Derek muttered. "Long time no see."

"You son of a gun!" Moose stepped closer. "You're the only one who ever got away from me!"

"I never admitted that it was me."

"And I blew out my damn knee before I got close enough to see your face," Moose poked Derek in the chest. "But I got a real good look of an Ethan North sweatshirt, just like that!"

"I've felt bad about that for years. I'm sorry."

"Sorry doesn't cut it with the Pennsylvania State Police. You should have turned yourself in."

"You would have confiscated my rifle."

"I sure would have. That's the law."

"Well … I couldn't let you do that."

"I see. Now, you hear me well, Derek Yeager. I have two open files on my desk that I'd like to close before I retire. That's one of them."

Derek shrugged.

"The other one is the disappearance of Cadet Jonathan Chen. Derek, you're going to help me close both of them before you get out of Parsons County again. I promise you that!"

———

Saturday supper was fried chicken, mashed potato and string beans, with apple pie for dessert.

A cold rain pelted the tall windows lining the dining hall. It was dark outside, but the art deco chandeliers illuminated the white tablecloths on the rows of empty tables, except where the old cadets and Lulu sat in one corner.

Their mood was somber. Derek and Kevin kept muttering about tearing Nob Hill village down plank by plank, but the remainder of the group felt that their chances of finding Jonathan were slipping away. Losing him was bad enough, but the new reality—that the dining hall might remain empty forever, and that the campus might settle into disused ruins on a hillside—was becoming apparent.

"The school wasn't going to make it, anyway," Walter rued. "Was it?"

"Not without a miracle," the colonel admitted. "Enrollment was falling to untenable levels, even before Jonathan went missing."

"What went wrong?" Kevin wondered aloud. "It was always teenage love-hate. But in the end, I have great memories of this place, even if I haven't come back to visit for a long time."

"That's part of the problem," Rocky reproached them. "You all went your own ways and forgot about this place."

"I know," Walter revealed. "Now I feel guilty for not staying connected. Maybe we could have saved Ethan North if we had paid closer attention to our alma mater."

Colonel Hammond cleared his throat for a pronouncement.

"It was the parents," Trip mused, uncharacteristically. "Boys have always loved it here. But today's parents balk at the small dorm rooms and the open bathrooms. And they hate the idea of cleaning duties being assigned to cadets. Parents today want prestige for their sons. And they want them pampered. Our rough-and-tumble way of life and old-fashioned values are hopelessly out of date."

"Exactly," Rocky stated. "These parents don't want their sons to stand on their own two feet. They want *advocates* to do the heavy lifting. Honor and self-respect are too hard, when you can buy good legal counsel, and judge self-worth by the amount of stuff you accumulate."

"It's all about denial and *bling* nowadays," Kevin nodded.

"There's my answer," Walter nodded. "Ethan North was the school that time forgot."

Derek sat farthest from Colonel Trip Hammond, with Lulu next to him.

"What was that exchange with the trooper all about?" Lulu whispered when she passed the string beans.

"It was nothing," Derek muttered.

Kevin sat across from Lulu, and he cast his eyes down when Derek dismissed her query.

Derek put his silverware down. Everyone except Kevin and the colonel had stopped eating. Rocky, Walter, and Lulu were looking at him.

"Colonel Hammond," Derek finally said, "might I have a word with you in your office after dinner?"

"Certainly," Trip Hammond said as he spooned mashed potatoes on his plate, and the meal resumed.

———

"You're coming with me," Derek said, after dessert.

"I know," Kevin muttered as he slowly took the four steps from the dining room up to the office level of Founders Hall.

"I'll wait for you in '51," Lulu suggested.

"No," Derek smiled. "I haven't answered your question yet. And I only want to do this once. So come in with us."

Colonel Hammond was standing behind his desk when they came in.

"What do you want to tell me, Derek?"

"It was me," Derek stood across the desk. "I did it. I shot that rabbit, and I'm sorry."

"And you lied about it," Colonel Hammond nodded. "That was the part that hurt you the worst."

"Yes, sir."

"I lied, too," Kevin uttered, feeling unsteady on his one leg.

"Yes. I know that you did, Kevin."

For a long time, Trip Hammond looked at the old cadets and nothing was said.

"Okay," Liu Chen spoke in her soft voice, "if you boys are all done with your moment of truth, or whatever you call this little ritual, will one of you please tell me what this is all about?"

"Let's all have a seat," Trip Hammond said.

They pulled up chairs, and Derek spoke.

"I used to keep a .22 rifle under my bed in Building '51," he said. "It was a present from my favorite uncle after my father died. It had been my father's gun when he was a kid, and it was my first gun. I just loved being outdoors with it."

"I don't get that at all," Lulu shrugged. "It must be a boy thing."

"Not entirely," Kevin piped up. "There are a whole bunch of country girls who feel that way, too."

"I still have that gun, Lulu. To this day, I've never shot a damn thing with it that I didn't eat after. Except for the squirrels and rabbits I gave to Boomer, up on Dynamite."

"So, you got expelled for keeping a gun in your dorm room?"

"No. I had to leave here because a state trooper … Moose … saw me shoot a rabbit for Boomer's stewpot. He chased me, and I only got away because he hurt his knee when he slipped on the hillside."

"Then how did you get implicated?"

"Moose Langdon limped off the mountain and drove himself to the emergency room. He came to Ethan North the next day since he'd seen my sweatshirt. Of course, Colonel Hammond knew I was the guilty party. Nobody spent as much time in the forest as me. But by then, my rifle was very well hidden in the attic crawl space of '51."

"And everybody knew that Derek and I didn't have any secrets," Kevin muttered. "Of course, I knew. We were roommates."

"Yes," Trip agreed. "You were always good friends."

"You know," Derek reflected. "Looking back on it, I stormed out of this office. But I'm not sure I ever heard you say that I was expelled."

"I was getting around to it," Trip offered, "but I was giving you one last chance if you recall. I don't believe that I actually said it at that point, either."

"I've always hoped that you didn't quit to take the heat off me,"

Kevin said. "I graduated under a cloud, to be sure. But I graduated with our class."

"I left because I didn't want to lose that .22 rifle. It was really important to me. Still is, in fact."

"That doesn't seem fair," Liu Chen spoke up. "No offense, Kevin. But you violated the honor code. Why should you have been able to graduate?"

"Miss Chen," Trip cleared his throat. "The honor code is a personal commitment to one's self."

"Explain, please," she doubted.

"We have never, ever, played boys against each other. When we talk about building character, we are talking about building lifelong friendships. There is no meaningful character in any of our lives without the support of others who share the same values. That is the one thing we hope young men leave here with."

"You don't say it that way in the cadet handbook," Derek muttered.

"The most important things are often left unsaid," Trip's eyes narrowed.

"I guess we didn't give you enough credit," Kevin said.

"Speaking of credit," Trip stood up and went to the storage closet. He rummaged around out of sight for a few seconds before emerging with a cardboard tube. "Do you want this now? Or should I save it for a more formal occasion?"

"What? My diploma?"

"You have now fulfilled the final requirements of an Ethan North graduate." Colonel Arthur C. W. Hammond III withdrew the ribbon-bound document from the container. "Congratulations."

CHAPTER 5

THE ELMS

Sunday breakfast was cold cereal, a banana, and toast.

They were pouring milk on their cereal and putting jelly on their toast when Leroy Jenks called from Nob Hill.

"You better get right over here!" the caretaker said. "And bring the boy's mother!"

"What's going on, Leroy?" Rocky Chambers asked.

"The sisters are dead, that's what's going on! Found 'em cold as fish this morning, all three of 'em. And there's something else."

"Well?"

"That Chinese boy was here, sure as the sun rises in the east. He's gone now, but he was here, all along. God help me, the kid was right here!"

"We're on our way, Leroy," Rocky Chambers said, to end the call. Then he spoke to the table. "We might be close to finding Jonathan. And he may be alive, apparently."

"Jonathan!" Liu Chen shouted, suddenly convulsed with emotion.

"Praise God!" Walter offered, with an enormous sigh of relief.

Liu Chen felt faint when they all pushed their chairs back, and Derek held her up.

"I'm coming with you," Colonel Trip Hammond stood with the group.

"Good," Rocky said. "Let's go."

"Wait for me," Kevin struggled to stand and get to the stairs at the front of Founders Hall.

"Kevin, we can't leave the campus unattended," Trip offered, going up the stairs. "The alumni association will be meeting at the museum today. Can you stay?"

"I guess I'd only slow you down," he reluctantly agreed.

Then Kevin surprised them all by drawing his Glock pistol. Only Derek knew that he was carrying it, and Kevin offered it to him.

"You might need this more than me, Derek."

"No, why don't you hang on to that, KO. Just don't shoot any schoolboys, okay?"

"No problem," Kevin glumly said as he re-holstered his weapon.

They left Kevin and piled into the school van, with Colonel Hammond and Rocky up front.

"You should have taken the gun away from Kevin," Lulu said, sitting between Derek and Walter as the van sped out between the lanterns on the stone wall at the front gate. "He's not well."

"He's still a cop, Lulu," Derek smiled, twisting on the bench seat to reach into his pocket. "And because I love Kevin like a brother ... I thumbed these out of the magazine while he was sleeping last night."

When he opened his fist, he held all twelve rounds of .40 caliber ammunition from Kevin's pistol in his palm.

———

Pigs were wandering everywhere when the group arrived at Nob Hill. The pigsty was open and Leroy Jenks was trying to herd the swine back into their enclosures.

Doc Humbolt's Buick was parked in front of the women's house.

"They've been dead a few hours," the doctor said when he greeted them at the door. "It looks like Diana and the other one poisoned themselves after Sister Sarah's heart gave out."

"What was it?" Walter asked.

"Whort root, I suspect," Doc Humbolt shrugged. "They've been boiling and refining it on the woodstove for days."

"Jonathan!" Liu Chen called into the house. "Where are you, Jon-Jon!"

"Take a look in the attic," the doctor offered.

Derek and Lulu raced up the stairways, with Rocky Chambers in hot pursuit. The post and beam frame of the dwelling was fully exposed on the top floor, and every item stored up there was neatly arranged. The only thing which was not perfectly in place was an angled door opening to a space in an alcove under the eaves, behind a brick chimney.

"What in hell?" Derek's fists clenched when he looked inside.

There was a small window in the space and a passage for food and a slop bucket.

"This is a hidden prison," Rocky uttered, holding one of the cattle prods he found outside the door. "There were always rumors that the Nobbers would lock away the unrepentant, or the disobedient."

A heavy barrel-top trunk inside had been pulled aside to reveal several loose floorboards leading to an even smaller space.

"Jonathan was probably in here when the FBI searched the place," Rocky muttered, "and he was probably heavily sedated."

"How could the feds miss a whole room?" Derek wanted to know.

"Those trunks and cases were probably piled in this alcove. And remember, the courts didn't give them much time to search the entire compound."

Liu Chen was in shock. Her mouth was moving, but no words were coming.

"Come on," Derek held her. "There's not a moment to waste."

Walter and Trip Hammond were waiting downstairs.

"It looks like they freed Jonathan before they ended their own lives," Rocky said. "He may not have gone far."

"Not with feral pigs in the woods, and the pens all opened up," Leroy Jenks regretted.

Liu Chen was sobbing and leaning on Derek.

"Jonathan is fast enough and smart enough to deal with them," the hunter uttered.

"He must be near here somewhere," Lulu sobbed. "My baby! He's probably scared to death. We've got to find him!"

"He would have made a dash for the safest place," Trip Hammond knew. "Ethan North Academy."

"Right. Except that it was pitch black and raining last night," Walter reminded them.

When a State Police cruiser pulled up in front of the house, Moose Landon got out wearing his trooper jacket and gun belt over jeans and a flannel shirt.

"Leroy, why are all these people here? I came as quick as I could after you called."

"Sorry, Moose. I thought that the mother needed to know first."

"The mother?"

"They were holding the Chinese kid in a hidden room upstairs," Leroy pleaded. "He's gone now. But honest to God, Moose, until today I never knew that room was there."

"Okay, I'll check it out," Moose headed for the stairs. "Now listen, all of you. This is a crime scene. None of you can leave. And for God's sake, don't touch a damn thing!"

Rocky pulled Derek and Trip aside as soon as Moose was upstairs.

"If Jonathan is running back to the school—if he makes it past the feral pigs and doesn't fall off some cliff—Kevin O'Connor is the only one there."

"You're right," Trip nodded. "Who knows how Kevin will react when some wild-eyed kid comes running up to him?"

"Let's go, Derek," Rocky said.

"Doc Humbolt's car?"

They inched away from the group and then made a mad dash for the Buick.

"Hey!" Moose called after them, coming back down the stairs.

"You can't leave here!"

By then, they were in the shiny sedan. In true Parsons County tradition, the keys were in the ignition, and Rocky Chambers drove away from Nob Hill with dirt flying from the tires.

———

After the others left him alone in Founders Hall, Kevin O'Connor took the golf cart to the mansion next door. The Elms had been Colonel Jacob North's home when he founded Ethan North Academy. A brick country home, with a wide porch and tall windows and ceilings. Every president of the school had lived there until it was too big and too drafty for Trip Hammond's young family. Now it was a museum with a grand staircase, full of old uniforms, pictures, and memorabilia.

He walked through the display cases and past the pictures and then looked outside. When the kitchen staff departed, Kevin knew that he was completely alone on the campus.

I wonder what will happen to this place, Kevin wondered as he turned back to the museum. *Will these rooms stay open after the school is torn down to make way for condos? Will alumni and tourists wander in here years from now to remember the last military prep school in America?*

The Gold Star Platoon memorial held a special place of honor across from the front door. Ethan North boys who had died in wars. Kevin had seen it many times, but when he stepped closer, the first name struck him with awe.

MARCUS BAKER, '14. ARGONNE FOREST.

That can't be, Kevin's brain stammered. *The battle of the Argonne was—what?—1918?*

Unless I met the grandson down in the tunnel. Maybe this is Mark Baker's grandfather—great grandfather—who died in World War I.

But Trip said...

Kevin rushed from picture to picture on the walls, pushing himself clumsily on his titanium leg. He knew that there must be a picture of Marcus Baker somewhere. He glanced at the only known photograph of Ethan North himself, a small portrait photograph in which the boy had slightly parted lips—the exhaling expression of the times—and hair parted in the middle. There were others, and when he found Marcus Baker, his own jaw dropped.

It was the boy from the tunnel.

No doubt about it.

Kevin sat down on one of the leather couches nearby. His missing limb was wracked with pain, and he fumbled with the pills before he swallowed them.

"Get a grip," he told himself out loud, and then mumbled. "Lots of times ... seen these names and pictures lots of times ... just my imagination ... fooling myself ..."

He looked around to get his bearings. There was a small brass plaque above the back of the leather couch, which said, "Placed here by the family of Matthew Greene, 1885–1898."

"No way," Kevin muttered and stood up. "No freaking way. It couldn't be ..."

He limped and stumbled around the museum, stamping hard on his artificial leg, tripping over displays and knocking over furniture, until he found a tiny sepia photograph of Matthew Greene on the wall. The years of his brief life were listed again, and someone had written "Influenza" across the bottom of the print in cursive ink, long ago.

It was absolutely the boy from the quarry.

"Air," Kevin muttered, "all I need is fresh air."

He limped out to the front porch and inhaled deeply. The air was different from Boston, fresh and clean, and the many elm trees on the wide lawns were in their full autumn glory.

He laughed, even though the pain in his stump of a leg was then excruciating.

"Bad enough my body is shot," Kevin said to no one, "now my mind is wasted."

He was looking across the lawn at the junior school—the oldest building, with a cupola on top—when the boy came running out the front door.

"You're not real," Kevin whispered, shaking his head, when the youth ran past the front porch of the Elms. Leaves began to fall heavily as he passed. He wore a white track shirt, brown leather cleats, and his hair, which was parted in the middle, flopped like wings as he ran.

"Hey, you!" Kevin called. "Stop! I want to ask you a question."

"Sorry! We're late."

"Who's late?"

"Come on. Hurry up!"

The roller coaster of Kevin's emotions dipped to despair and anger, and for a moment, he touched the butt of his Glock and thought about shooting this youth, like a fleeing felon.

"What are you waiting for?" the kid turned around and said with a big smile. "Come on, let's go."

Kevin saw Rocky's pickup truck at Founders Hall. He hopped over to it, falling once on the concrete walkway and skinning his left knee—his only flesh-and-bone knee—badly enough that traces of blood appeared on his chinos.

The keys were in the ignition, but when he reached for the pedals with his foot, Kevin realized that he wouldn't be able to drive the standard transmission. Not safely, at least. But he started the truck's engine anyway and figured a way to combine the clutch and the accelerator and the parking brake into some semblance of driving.

He turned the wheel to aim the truck towards the front gate and put it in gear. Rolling downhill, he put it in second.

The boy was outside the main gate, striding across the street to the soccer field. Kevin pursued him across the pitch to the edge of the trees, then down a trail until it became too narrow. Then he cut out onto a back road on the edge of town and back up another trail.

Without a seatbelt on the rough trails, he was sliding all over the truck's bench seat. But Kevin didn't care, he was laughing by then, thrilled by the joy of driving again. He was no longer lying in rehabilitation, being rolled over by nurses to do his business in a bedpan. He was no longer watching his left leg atrophy to a twig, while his right leg swelled and putrefied in the splint which was holding the mismatched bones and muscles and skin in place. He was in pursuit, like a lawman once again, and he would catch this offender and solve the mystery and they would return Jonathan Chen to his mother. Perhaps he would even wheel the Bomb Squad truck through the streets to rescue the city one more time.

He was a hero once again.

Kevin could barely see the kid running across fields and through the forest, but he knew all the tricks of pursuit, all the *zigs* and *zags* and feints and tricks which a person in flight might try. So when the kid crossed a cornfield and ran to the far side, Kevin intercepted him.

"Stop! Talk to me!"

The kid was laughing and running alongside the driver's door of Rocky's truck, his collar just out of reach, until he clambered up a slope at the far end. There, he stopped and turned back to Kevin.

"What's the matter? Can't you get up here?"

Kevin got out of the truck. He had a hard time just standing in the clumpy, uneven field. But he faced the kid, ten feet away.

"What are you afraid of, kid?"

"I fear nothing," the boy boasted.

"Then come down here. I won't hurt you."

The kid cocked his head with a questioning look.

"Why don't you come up here?"

"I can't. You have to come down here."

"Can't? I thought you were an Ethan North boy? *You can if you think you can.*"

"Listen, kid. I realized a long time ago that those platitudes are bullshit. I only have one leg. I know I can't get up there."

"Are you sure you're an Ethan North boy?" the kid mocked. "*Winners never quit, quitters never win.*"

"I'm not quitting. I can't do it to start with."

"*Dress like a champion, act like a champion, be a champion.*"

"Stop quoting that nonsense, kid. That crap doesn't cut it, in the real world."

The boy was standing on a high trail along the edge of the field. When Kevin tried to climb up to him, he went to the next higher level.

"Who are you? By the way, you're wearing my old athletic number on that shirt. Who the hell are you?"

Kevin crawled up the dirt slope, grabbing roots and rocks to pull himself higher. At the top, Kevin made a desperate grab for his ankle.

Lacking a useful rotator cuff in his right shoulder, Kevin couldn't hold on to the boy.

"Hey!" the youth pulled away. "Don't be like that!"

"You're not even real. What do you care?"

"No? Remember this game? All cadets played it."

The boy leaned down and took a swipe at Kevin's face, but he pulled back and stopped his hand.

"Ha! Ha! You flinched!" the boy said, and punched Kevin's arm. Not hard. But a fist definitely landed on Kevin's biceps with a thump.

"You were the boy in the service tunnel! Weren't you? And at the quarry. You're all one, aren't you?"

"No. You know who those boys were."

"No! They weren't Marcus Baker and Matthew Greene. How could that be?"

"Sometimes, old cadets come back, when they are needed."

Kevin pulled himself up to the boy's level, but they were in a thicket, and there was not enough strength in his sound leg to stand.

"No one can come back from the grave, kid."

"I call them and they come. But only the ones who are young enough to remember."

"Remember what?"

"What Ethan North Academy was all about."

"Ha! That's a laugh. Why don't you tell me? Because I was at Ethan North for five years, and sometimes my head hurts when I try to fathom what it was all about. Other than having a lot of fun with Derek and the guys, getting a diploma, and getting the hell away from the place."

"What was fun about that?"

"Come on, now. The place was so ridiculous we had to laugh about it. The meals were scanty and the rooms were tiny cubicles. We ran from chapel to class to drill all day long. We didn't have decent athletic uniforms, but that didn't matter since we were too small a school to put together powerhouse teams."

"My heart bleeds purple piss for you," the kid laughed.

"Fact is, we were a poor school. It was all about keeping the tuition as low as possible, almost as low as if we stayed at home. Otherwise, most of us wouldn't have been there. Isn't that what Ethan North Academy was all about?"

"Who taught you how to shine your shoes and stand up straight? Who showed you how to get your algebra homework done, Kevin, and how to pass the daily quizzes that Coach gave in his American History class? Who told you to wash your face before your ass in the shower?"

"Other cadets, I guess."

"That's right. The older boys always brought the younger ones along. It was never the teachers who showed you *how to learn, how to labor and how to live.* It was the corps of cadets, as a body, who raised each other higher. It was that way for a hundred and sixteen years. The same drill, the same jokes, the same games. Don't let it end here."

Kevin managed to stand when the boy took his hand and helped him pull himself up. Eye to eye, he knew who this was, if only from the picture.

"Ethan? You're Ethan North, aren't you?"

"Hello, Kevin."

"This isn't happening. You're not real. Ethan North has been dead a hundred and sixteen years. Who are you?"

"Look at where we are, Kevin."

"Wait ... I know this place. These fields on top of the hill go almost all the way back to the school."

"You don't remember?"

"I'm not sure ... but ... I think that one time when I ran through here ... alone ... I found an old kiln built into the hillside. It's hard to see ... I never found it again, no matter how many times I came back with Derek to show it to him ... but it's right around here ..."

Kevin tried to take a step but fell and landed on his side in the vines. He landed nearly face down in a crumbling brick-lined hole.

"Why…"

"Ha! Ha!" Ethan North laughed. "You were never the best boy at school. But you turned out to be a good man, Kevin O'Connor."

Kevin hung his head over the rim of the kiln's chimney.

Something—someone—was in there.

Someone had fallen in and was badly hurt. Moaning, so weakly, far below in the darkness. Kevin O'Connor knew the pain well enough to sense it at a distance.

He looked up again, ready to tell the running boy to summon the help which he could not provide. He was helpless and lying in the box huckleberry at the edge of the ancient kiln, and Ethan North was gone.

———

"Where the hell is Kevin?"

Derek came out of the Elms after looking through the museum. The golf cart was there, but there was no sign of his old roommate.

"My truck is gone," Rocky said. "I left it right alongside Founders Hall."

"We've got to find him before he finds Jonathan. Let's go to your farm, Rocky."

"I know what you're thinking," Rocky said as they got back into the Buick, "but this weather is horrible."

"It's clearing. I can cover a lot of territory with the Cessna. I should be able to spot your truck easily. And I might even get sight of Jonathan if he's out there."

"Look," Rocky pointed outside as he drove, "the top of Dynamite is in the clouds. And there's patchy fog in the valleys. You don't stand a chance in crappy weather like this."

"I'll be okay," Derek nodded.

They jumped out of Doc Humbolt's car at Rocky's farm. When Derek climbed into the Cessna, he was surprised to see Rocky getting into the right seat.

"Four eyes are better than two," Rocky muttered, well aware of the danger.

"Let's hope this thing starts," Derek said as he stroked the primer and cracked open the throttle. When he engaged the starter, the propeller flicked by in front of the cowling. Then the six big cylinders of the Continental engine roared with power.

The grass was wet and smooth when they took off into the misty sky.

"We'll just fly down the valley to the river," Derek said, with the fields and trees a few hundred feet under their wings. The sky was a gray shroud above them. They couldn't actually discern the bottoms of the clouds, but when Derek climbed too high, the world disappeared in ragged mist. Then he descended slightly, and they were under the weather again.

The brick buildings and trees of Ethan North Academy on the side of Dynamite Mountain were even with their wings when they flew over New Manor. They followed Newport Road, towards the fossil pits and Nob Hill.

"There's my truck!" Rocky pointed to a wooded hillside cut with trails.

"I don't have room to come around for another look," Derek said. "We'll have to go down to the river and do a one-eighty."

They flew past Nob Hill and turned down the Little Juniata River.

"Aren't there power lines across the river somewhere?" Derek peered out the windshield.

"Down!" Rocky said.

Derek felt Rocky nudge the yoke forward. He heeded the warning and flew a few feet above the rushing water as the red warning balls on high tension lines passed over the top of their wings.

"Okay," Derek gulped, "let's take another look."

He banked the wings back towards New Manor, and they flew up the valley.

"Low cloud ceilings and rising terrain," Rocky warned. "This is bad business, Derek."

"Just another day in Alaska," Derek muttered. He flew the Cessna so smoothly that it felt like they were sitting in their own living rooms, even in the turns. Only the trees and houses passing close under the wings made it obvious that their perch was precarious.

They roared above Nob Hill and the fossil pits. Rocky could see the rest of their group looking up from the village as they sped by.

"There he is!" Rocky called, a few seconds later. "That's Kevin on the ground, a little uphill from my truck!"

"We can turn around on the other side of town," Derek said. "Got your cell phone?"

"I'm on it," Rocky said as he dialed Trip Hammond's number.

Derek turned the Cessna around in the wider valley west of New Manor. When he came around towards the river again, he dropped ten degrees of flaps and started to slow the airplane.

"You're not..." Rocky uttered.

"Yes I am. I think I can make that field on the hilltop. Give me full flaps when I call for them."

"You're going to be half in the clouds up there," Rocky readied his hand on the flap switch. "I'm getting that old funny feeling I used to get when the enemy was close."

"Yup," Derek said as he slowed the Cessna and skimmed the trees on the hillside. There were still some autumn leaves on the branches and their colors seemed to blend into a sloppy mousse as they sped by in the mist, that close.

"Now!" Derek called as they cleared a tree line. "Full flaps!"

He cut the power and the Cessna dropped towards a cornfield. The stalks had been cut, and luckily, they were lined up with the furrows.

They landed on all three wheels and when they bounced, Derek pushed the yoke forward to replant the main wheels and keep the tail wheel up. He cut the engine before they were stopped, upright and unscathed.

"Nice work," Rocky said as he climbed out.

"I'd rather be lucky than good, any day," Derek said as they took off running among the furrows.

The two men clambered down the hillside. They saw the truck first, and then found Kevin nearby, lying in a thicket of vines.

"He's down here!" Kevin's shoulders were hanging over the rim at the top of the kiln. "He's alive, but we have to get him out of there, right now!"

"Easy, Kevin," Rocky said. "Let us take a look."

"Jonathan?" Derek called down, wondering if this was another of Kevin's illusions.

"I'm here," a weepy voice answered. "Please. It hurts."

"It's okay, Jonathan," Kevin called. "Help is coming. Hang on, buddy."

"The firebox!" Rocky said as he jumped to his feet. "We have to dig him out that way!"

Kevin stayed at the top when Derek and Rocky tumbled down the slope and began to pull rocks and debris away from the old lower opening to the kiln. Their efforts were frantic but effective.

"Damn it," Derek muttered, when three feral pigs circled menacingly in the brush nearby. "They must have been chasing this kid when he fell into the opening."

"Enough of that," Rocky Chambers spat as he reached down to his boot and pulled a pistol out of an ankle holster.

Rocky raised the pistol, aimed over the sights and fired three shots from the compact .45 in one smooth motion, and the pigs stumbled and fell hard in the underbrush.

"You don't mess around, do you?" Derek said, in awe of the old man's speed and accuracy.

"Keep digging," Rocky grunted as he pushed the pistol home into his favorite holster.

When the crew from Nob Hill Village arrived, the refrain was "Dig! Dig!" Walter Weiss and Trip Hammond joined Derek and Rocky, scooping dirt and stones and broken bricks out of the bottom opening of the kiln with their bare hands.

"Your mother is here!" Kevin said down the hole, when Liu Chen and Doc Humbolt climbed to the top opening.

"Mom!"

Liu Chen tried to dive into the opening at the top of the kiln headfirst to get to Jonathan until Kevin and Doc Humbolt grabbed her waist and held her back.

Kevin left Doc Humbolt with Lulu and rolled down the hill. He tried to stand, but his artificial leg was loose and falling off, held partially in place by his pants. Then he looked and saw the New Manor Volunteer Fire Department arriving in force. State Police cruisers, the ambulance corps, and farmers' trucks came across the fields and through the forest.

In the distance, the Ethan North bell tower chimed the hour.

When Kevin looked up, the rain had stopped, and high canyons of golden sunshine were cleaving apart the clouds.

CHAPTER 6

LAST TRAIN HOME

"I thought I left here for the last time once before."

Derek Yeager stood in their room that Monday morning, stuffing his gear into his duffel bag.

"Yeah," Kevin agreed. "I left here under a dark cloud, twenty years ago. Because my best friend had been expelled two weeks earlier."

"We're all good now," Derek beamed. "I feel great about Ethan North Academy, now that Trip and I have worked things out."

"About time," Kevin laughed.

"I'm even going to get involved in remaking the school. Trip wants me to start an alumni outreach program. I agreed, as long as I can spend my summers in Alaska. How cool is that?"

"Will wonders never cease," Walter Weiss offered. He was standing in their open door, with his own suitcase. "Me too. I'm the new science teacher at Ethan North. Now all I have to do is go home and tell my family why we're moving to Pennsylvania."

When the three old cadets walked across the campus with their traveling bags, they found Rocky standing with Trip in front of Founders Hall.

"Any word on Jonathan?" Walter asked the older men.

"He's going to survive," Trip nodded. "But his injuries may be disabling."

"What did the Nobbers want with him, anyway?" Derek wanted to know.

"They read him Bible verses and spoke to him in tongues all day long," Rocky shrugged. "I suppose they believed they could convert him, and keep their stupid cult going."

"He'll be all right," Kevin said. "That kid is amazing. But what about the school? Is Ethan North going to make it?"

"We're inviting all of our students and teachers back." Colonel Arthur C. W. Hammond III beamed. "It'll be a slow start this year, but with the help of the alumni, we'll be back in operation."

"Even Liu Chen is talking about staying in Parsons County," Rocky said. "Jonathan is going to have a long recovery time from his injuries, but he told her that he'd like to be near his friends when Ethan North reopens."

"Too bad Lulu can't be here," Kevin regretted. "I'd like to say good-bye."

"You can come visit her at my camp in Alaska," Derek laughed. "She and Jonathan are coming up with me next summer."

"Good for you, Derek."

"Hop in my truck, Kevin," Rocky offered. "I'll give you a ride down to the train."

"Thanks. But I want to walk away from here on my own," Kevin said. Then he turned to Derek and Walter. "Come with me, guys?"

They walked down Carlisle Street and past the Soldiers and Sailors Monument in the center of New Manor.

"How's the pain, Kevin?"

"Oh, it doesn't matter."

"No drugs today?"

"I don't need them anymore. My head is clearer today than any time in the past year."

"One thing I have to know," Walter questioned, "how did you stumble onto that kiln?"

"I can't explain it," Kevin shrugged. "I'd forgotten all about that thing. I only saw it once, twenty-some-odd years ago, and never found it again."

"Well, perhaps the pain medications opened your mind to suggestion, and triggered a memory?"

"If that fits, it must be the explanation."

The rails began singing when they stood in the semi-abandoned station. A train was coming.

"So," Walter said, "will we see you next alumni weekend?"

"No. I think that this was my last visit. There's someplace I have to go."

"I know," Derek said, looking at his friend as if for the last time. "I think I've figured it out, Kevin. I know."

"Our secret, right?" Kevin smiled. "Don't snitch."

"I haven't figured this out at all," Walter doubted. "And there's one thing that really bothers me. Jonathan landed on his knees in the bottom of that kiln. The boy's right tibia plateau was shattered, his left leg was broken, and his right shoulder was severely dislocated. Those injuries are identical to yours, KO. That's … incredible."

The train stopped in front of them with the brakes screeching amid a hiss of compressed air.

"I'd call it a coincidence if I believed in coincidences." Kevin smiled and shook Walt's hand.

"Take care, KO," Derek said as Kevin climbed into the train and waved farewell to his friends. The train had a schedule to keep, and it began to move right away.

"So, they found that missing kid?" the conductor said. "That's amazing!"

"Yes," he shuffled to a seat. "It was."

"Were you involved in the rescue?"

"Not really. I'm just an old cadet who went back for one last look."

Kevin lowered himself into his seat. After the long walk, the phantom pains came in intense waves, but he didn't seem to mind.

The train rocked into the Kettle Mountain tunnel and he closed his eyes and smiled. The tingling came up his stump into his weak shoulder and spread through his broken body, not unpleasantly.

When the conductor came back through he thought that the man with the limp had to be in the dining car or the lavatory. So the railroad man moved on and didn't give it much thought, since passengers wandered around from car to car all the time and the man's fare was paid all the way to the end of the line at Boston. But in the light of day on the other side of the Kettle Mountain tunnel and the Little Juniata trestle, that seat was empty.

ONE YEAR LATER

EPILOGUE

Leaves were falling from the trees again at the start of the following alumni weekend, when the new corps of cadets marched around the quad and down to the parade grounds for the homecoming muster.

"It's a shame Kevin couldn't be here," Lulu said, walking towards the parade grounds between Derek and Walter.

Derek answered her, but only halfheartedly.

"Once the infection came back and spread to his bloodstream…"

His hand was on her lower back under her long black ponytail.

"Still, it would have been nice if Jonathan could have known the man who saved him," Lulu smiled. "Kevin left New Manor so abruptly last year."

Derek's hand slipped off her back when she moved ahead of the two men, catching up to Jonathan and his friends. He was seventeen then, and moving adroitly on his artificial right leg. In a move which helped to bolster enrollment, Ethan North Academy had taken Jonathan Chen and several other New Manor residents as day students.

The two old cadets were left alone when they stopped to allow the drum and bugle corps to pass ahead.

"Shouldn't we tell her?"

"She's a scientist," Derek rued. "She would never accept it."

"I'm a scientist," Walter noted, "and I can't accept it."

"Lulu would never let it go. She'd go crazy trying to solve a thing that can't be solved."

"Yes. I have to believe that someday, the horizons of science will advance far enough to include this sort of phenomena. But right now, we'd be considered crazy if we ever went public with it."

"We have to take it as a gift," Derek smiled.

They were bringing up the rear in the throng of alumni who had walked down to the parade grounds. The large number of old cadets attending the homecoming gave them all new hope that Ethan North Academy might still be saved.

"Don't you feel guilty about falsifying the date in his obituary for the alumni bulletin?"

"Not a bit," Derek mused.

"Still ... it couldn't be! We talked to him. We broke bread with him in the dining hall. And how did Rocky's truck get to the kiln if someone didn't drive it there?"

"An illusion could not have caught the bottle of Birch Beer I tossed to Kevin, either. But someone did. And Doc Humbolt certainly would have known if he wasn't examining flesh and blood."

"There has to be an explanation."

"There is no explanation. Kevin O'Connor died fourteen months ago, in the VA hospital in Baltimore, from lingering wounds suffered in the bomb blast. We both saw the death certificate. The date was not a misprint."

"So who was that we saw here twelve months ago?"

Derek shrugged. He had no words.

"Rocky and Trip should know," Walter Weiss insisted.

"Rocky never really believed that I saw Boomer, back in the day. This would be too fantastic for his military mind."

"Even so, our former teachers should know."

"How do we do that, Walt? How do we tell them that when we

tried to invite Kevin to homecoming this year, we discovered that he had died two months before we saw him here last alumni weekend?"

It was Walter's turn to answer with a shrug.

"All I know for sure is that we know something that is meant only for us," Derek Yeager offered. "Only for our gang in '51."

They both looked up the hill to their old dormitory.

"We did grow up in a world of our own up there," Walter said.

"Don't you remember the first rule for cadets, Walter? The rule that applied whenever one of us pulled off some harmless stunt or prank which would go forever unsolved by the school's administration?"

"Sure, I do."

Don't snitch.

www.dscooperbooks.com